COME HELL OR HIGH WATER

THE WATER TRILOGY | BOOK THREE

BRITNEY KING

WWW.BRITNEYKING.COM

ALSO BY BRITNEY KING

Water Under The Bridge

Dead In The Water

The Social Affair

Bedrock

Breaking Bedrock

Beyond Bedrock

Around The Bend

Somewhere With You

Anywhere With You

COME HELL OR
HIGH WATER

BRITNEY KING

COPYRIGHT

Hot Banana Press

Cover Design by Britney King LLC

Cover Image by Ivan Vander Biesen

Copy Editing by Librum Artis Editorial Services

First Edition: 2017

ISBN: 978-0-9966497-9-7 (Paperback)

ISBN: 978-0-9966497-5-9 (All E-Books)

britneyking.com

For the readers—
It all started with a book.

PREFACE

There's a woman not long dead
who rests down
by the water's edge.
Her final words were,
"Please. Just get it over —"
She never did get the second half
of her sentiment out.
I made sure she never would.
Some things are best left unsaid.
In the end, it didn't matter anyhow.
I knew she was ready to die.
And she knew it, too.

❧

There's a woman who rests down
by the water's edge.
She wasn't good for us,
but you tried to make it okay.
It cost us—that's on you.
I knew keeping her was wrong.
I just wish you had, too.

❧

CHAPTER ONE

KATE

AFTER

Life often has a funny way of leading you around to where it wants you to be, at least that's what I've come to find. Speaking of finding things, I know I shouldn't be here. It was a risky move, coming, but at the same time—a promise is a promise. I said I'd take care of this, and I'm determined to hold up my end of the deal. Still, that doesn't mean I have to like it.

Get in. Get out. I repeat this to myself over and over, step by step, until I reach the front porch. When my foot hits the first stair, I pause and glance backward over my shoulder. I just need a moment. The sun is bright today, but the sun is deceptive. It isn't warm; there's a chill in the air, and it's the kind that stings when it hits my skin. The wind whips my hair, covering my face; it has little concern for anything that stands in its way. I brush it back and climb the remaining steps. If only it weren't so cold out. I might've stayed put; I might've changed my mind. I might've gone back home to you.

Ring the bell, I say to myself. *Lift your finger and push the bell.* I know what to do; I just can't make myself do it. Thankfully, the decision is made for me. Before I gather the nerve to press the bell, the door swings open, and something shifts —and it isn't the wind. It's something within me, and that something feels a whole lot like my resolve. I swallow hard, trying to dislodge the lump that's formed in my throat. It doesn't help. Turns out, a little saliva has nothing on fear, and so the lump remains. Also, I'm standing face to face with him, and it feels like a long time coming.

Up close, he's different than I imagined. That's not to say that I really imagined much. I guess I'd just expected a little more from her, is all. Someone not so... ordinary looking, would be one way to put it. If this is her type, then what do I know? Maybe it's the gray that peppers the dark hair at his temples, or maybe it's the way his smile turns downward, but he seems older than I thought he'd be.

He doesn't speak immediately. He greets me with a nod, and we stare at each other in some sort of silent standoff, sizing one another up, or at least I assume that's what we're doing. I wonder if he can read the sleepless nights on my face, or see the effects of the twelve pounds that I've lost in just two weeks alone. Can he see the guilt in my ashen face? Can he feel the sadness in the pit of my stomach? Does he see the despair in my eyes? Does he know that I'm a failure, as a mother, a wife, a friend? If he can, he doesn't say. He simply moves to the side, allowing me to slip by and into his world as though we've known each other our whole lives.

For a moment, I consider that he isn't the man I've come to see. But as I pass, I notice in his expression a mild curiosity, the kind she described, and I realize it's definitely him. Also, that I shouldn't have come.

What are you doing, Kate? It's your voice, not mine, that I hear and it suddenly becomes clear—really clear—that no

8

one knows I'm here. Still, I can't help myself. I showed up for a reason, and I know I won't be able to forgive myself if I don't see this through, and so when he rounds the corner, and he beckons me to follow, I do. Better to get it over with and get on with your day, his posture seems to say.

The inside of the place is darker and stuffier than it looked from the outside. I was pleased to see when I Googled the address, that he offices out of an old home. I've always had a thing for old houses, and this one does not disappoint. From the curb, it is apparent it is well kept, but in here, it feels empty—lonely—in need of something I can't quite name. *Just like her.*

Making my way through the hall, I wonder if he lives here, in this old house, with the loneliness and the unname-able things. I almost ask, but he ushers me into our final destination, a second living area which has been converted into an office, and I think better of it. The room is smartly decorated, which makes sense, considering his connection to her. But maybe I'm projecting. If so, I've certainly come to the right place. I laugh softly at the thought, maybe because I'm nervous, or maybe it's the book that catches my eye.

In any case, there's not much to the space, aside from a desk, a small couch, and an armchair. He clears his throat and then shuffles his feet, and it suddenly occurs to me that I haven't got all day, and I probably ought to get on with it.

He doesn't say so, but his straight back and upturned mouth give the impression that he holds all the answers one could ever need, tucked neatly into his back pocket, and it momentarily crosses my mind that maybe I don't really want to know them after all.

I can feel his eyes on me, which is why I meet his gaze. His expression appears to say that he expects I'll be comfort-able here, and I hope he is right. Does he know I can't decide whether I've come to kill him or simply to satisfy my curiosity? It's hard to say. What I do know is the intensity with which he studies me also makes me want to go, to press rewind and reverse every mistake I've likely just made by coming here. But I won't. I can't.

When I step further into the office, he follows. I glance toward his desk. I don't see any therapist-type things on it— there aren't files— and there aren't pens or notepads. Instead, it's covered in books, stacked neatly in rows. I inhale, and if life-changing had a scent, it would smell like this. It's *The Great Gatsby* that caught my eye. The irony of the past, beckoning. "It was my father's," he says, clearing his throat, and I don't know if he's referring to the book or the desk, and I don't ask.

I shift, but I make a mental note to get a better look at the selection of books he owns before our time is up. It's interesting; I don't know what I'll find on that desk, only that it'll be something brilliant, probably something a little uncomfortable, like *Lolita* or *The Scarlet Letter*, the type of book that stretches the reader. He sees me looking, and he smiles. I know that whatever is in those stacks, I won't find anything simple or cozy or sweet, but rather something in your face— direct— the kind of book that asks something of you. *Set your feelings aside*, it says. *Let me take the lead; I'll show you how this goes.*

He closes the door behind him, and I wonder whether this is customary—a convention to make me more comfortable— to get me to open up, because it doesn't appear there are any other occupants in the house. Also, up close, he's tall. Taller than I realized. Taller than you, even. He moves quickly across the room, like a cat, and takes a seat. He doesn't motion for me to sit; he just assumes I'll know what to do. He's all business, until he isn't.

"Would you care for something to drink?" he asks, raising his brow. "Tea? Coffee? Vodka?"

His voice is low; it resonates somewhere deep inside, bounces around and lodges itself just where it wants to be. Like yours. I glance at an imaginary watch on my wrist. "It's a little early for vodka," I say.

"Just barely," he tells me, and the words catch on his lips and hang there. I don't respond. I study his hands instead. They seem like capable hands—like yours, like hers, I think. He folds them in his lap; he isn't one for small talk. When I look up, I shift my focus to his face. I'm trying to get a sense of the direction he'll take, but all I see is nothing, and I can't guess which way things will go. *He knows her, too.* "So—Mrs. —"

"Water," I interject, and my voice comes out smooth, just the way I wanted it.

"Water. That's right. I remember now from your email," he says and then he pauses to look up at me, peering over his glasses as he does. "What an interesting name…" he adds and then he furrows his brow as though he's just remembered something long forgotten. I've seen that look before. You have it down to an art.

Still, he doesn't take his eyes off mine. "But I bet you've heard that before."

"A time or two, yes," I answer, averting my gaze. I don't mean to look away, but those eyes of his, they burn. They're the kind that see through you, and I don't particularly want to be seen through. He nods curtly, and he waits before he speaks again, although I'm not sure for what.

"Anyway," I say. "It's Ginny," I mention, because silence seems like the wrong way to go. I offer the name because I need something to fill the space, but also because it feels good rolling off my tongue. *Ginny.* It's a girlish name, one that reminds me of someone who's perpetually young— bright— sunny and happy. A person named Ginny could never do anything bad. I picture her in my mind. She would be nothing at all like me.

"Okay then, Ginny—" he starts. I know I am supposed to maintain eye contact, and so I do. It isn't easy. "You've come a long way," he says, and he's only partially right.

"Yes," I tell him.

"And you mentioned in your email that you have something of mine?"

"Yes," I say, bending down to remove the book from my bag. I look up at him, and suddenly it seems odd that he didn't ask for it at the door. But then, I knew he wouldn't. He may not be the kind for small talk, but he's not impolite either. He watches me carefully. I lean forward and hand it to him.

He takes it from me carefully, as though it might slip through his fingers. I watch as he studies the cover and flips it over in his hands. *"Lady Chatterley's Lover,"* he whispers, running his fingers along its edge. He glances up suddenly. "Where did you get this?"

"I found it on a bench in the park…"

"Which park?"

"Downtown."

He cocks his head. "Where downtown?"

"Lou Neff…"

"Huh," he says.

"I was running the trail—I stopped to stretch and there it was…"

He flips open to the title page. "And you saw my name here," he says pointing.

I grit my teeth. "I Googled you. I hope you don't mind."

"Not at all," he tells me and exhales. I hear relief in it. "This book is very special to me."

"I figured as much…" I say. "Seeing that your name is inside."

He looks away again, and it doesn't escape me that maybe he knows I'm lying.

"It says, *I love you always*. I figured it might've been a gift."

"Yes," he replies. "It was." I can see that he doesn't want to say more—that he isn't going to— but at the same time, I'm not ready for the conversation to end.

"I'm glad it's found its way back," I say.

He nods, I smile. "Anyway—seeing that you're a therapist and all, I was wondering if you might have time for a quick question?"

He nods once again, as though maybe he were expecting as much. He doesn't tell me I've come to the right place. He doesn't reassure me, not like most people would. He isn't trying to sell me, and I respect this about him.

"I've been wondering how one knows…" I start, and then I stop and twist my hair around one finger. I pull it tight and then let go. "I was wondering how one might know—or—rather, I guess what I'm trying to say is—" I pause to take a deep breath. "I was wondering how someone really knows when it's time to end a relationship."

He tilts his head, like this is the most interesting thing he's heard in a long time, when we both know it isn't. "That's an interesting question."

I offer a nervous smile. "An interesting question that has an answer?"

"Well," he begins, and he pauses to rub his jaw. "How long have you been asking yourself whether or not you should end things?"

"Eight months, two weeks, five days."

He raises his brow, drops his hand. "That's pretty exact."

"Yes."

"Are you always so precise?"

"Lately…"

"I see," he says. Then he narrows his eyes, his gaze boring holes through me. "And what would you say has changed?"

"Everything."

"I see," he tells me thoughtfully, but he's wrong. He doesn't see.

When I don't say anything he adjusts his glasses. "Do you want to extrapolate?" he asks, and there isn't any emotion on his face as he says it, and I want to know more about how he hides his emotions so well. All of a sudden, he reminds me of you, and I'm not sure what to make of this either. I'm not sure what I expected to find, coming here, only that somehow this revelation isn't helping any.

I shrug slightly and then tuck my hands between my thighs. "I just thought maybe there was a way to know…"

"Do you still love this person?"

"More than is good for me," I reply, and the words slice through my insides on their way out.

"And yet you feel unsure as to whether you want to stay in the relationship," he states. Then he pauses, again. He likes to leave space between his comments, crevices one can just fall into. It's a minefield, navigating all that space. It's a question, but not a question. It's brilliant, is what it is.

I nod my head. "Yes."

"May I ask why?"

"I guess you could say it's no longer compatible with my lifestyle." And there it is, each syllable taking all of me with them when they go. I don't know what I feel as they hang in the air between us. Maybe nothing. Maybe something. Maybe I just needed to say the words. Still, I wish I could take them back, suck them in, make it not so. But I can't. Turns out, most things, you can't take back—what's done is done.

"I'm sorry," he tells me, and it's genuine.

"Me too," I say, and I look away.

"Letting go of someone special can be very difficult."

I swallow hard, and the tears come even though I don't want them to. It's like everything that's happened—it all hits me at once, and I can't help it. Not this time. I wipe my cheek with the back of my hand and then I meet his eyes. "Tell me about it."

~

CHAPTER TWO

KATE

Before

I've been studying her for months. I know how she takes her coffee, the color she prefers on her nails, the way her mouth moves when she sleeps. I don't know what she looks like when she's happy. But I will.

That's not to say I meant to keep her this long. And, of course, you, well *you*, never intended to keep her at all. But then, what's done is done.

"I want you to be happy here," I told her the first week she was here, not long after we let the drugs wear off completely.

"I don't see how that's possible," she said.

"Tell me what makes you happy."

I could see her thinking about my question; I could see that I'd set something into motion. It wasn't immediate—most things that are truly great rarely are, but eventually her lips turned upward. Slowly, she broke out into a full-on smile, and it was like the sun coming out on a cloudy day. "He makes me happy."

"Your husband," I said. It wasn't a question. Mostly

because it hadn't occurred to me that it should be.

She laughed just slightly. The smile remained. "Something like that."

"I see," I told her, raising my brow.

She looked at me then, really looked at me. The smile faded but her eyes lit up. "Not yet, you don't," she said. "But you will."

I didn't reply. I'm not sure what I could have said that would have been appropriate in a moment like that. Still, I took it for what it was, a promise. Hope. Something for the future. She wasn't offering everything. But it wasn't nothing, either.

∾

It can take weeks, sometimes months, to break a person down. My father taught me that. It's why I'm doing all this. It's why I go to the lengths I go, to try and cheer her up. But I'd be lying if I said I was sure it's working. From the looks of her, I'm not so sure at all.

I watch her on the monitor as I always do before going in, studying her demeanor. From that vantage, I do my best to gauge her mood, to put myself in the right mindset to get what I want from her, to give her what she needs from me.

She looks up, and even though she can neither see nor hear me, she senses I'm there. It's easy for her, in a way. I visit every day at this time. I lean into the monitor to take a closer look, and I can't help but notice the way her collarbone juts out from her shoulder, the way it connects to her neck, and I wonder: Was it this pronounced yesterday?

She sits on the floor, just as she has since the day you put her here. I consider her position, her shoulders; they're squared in the oversized T-shirt she's wearing. But are they as squared as they were yesterday? The day before?

Six months ago, I purchased a size medium, but you wouldn't know it now. You'd think I bought an extra large the way it hangs off her now. The pajama bottoms are barely hanging on, just the same. Thinking about those pants, I remember how we argued over them, you and I. It was one of the few times we've fought since *before*. Since she's been in our lives. You didn't take it so well when I bought her these clothes. She isn't staying, you told me, but you didn't meet my eye when you said it, and now I wished you had. Maybe I should have challenged you more from the beginning, set some ground rules, but who could've known how good this would be for us.

I get chills when I think about it now. But it could be that it's cold in this room. It's always cold. It's this way on purpose, you say. We wouldn't want our captive getting too comfortable. Who could be comfortable in a 16x16 foot holding cell, I wanted to argue, but I didn't. Mostly because you're right. Also, we're on a winning streak, we're in our zone, and I refuse to be the one to mess that up.

The only trouble is that when it's good, it makes it easy to remember how bad it can get. It wasn't always this way, this seamless, but it was always a possibility. I see that now.

~

FROM THE BEGINNING, IT WAS SOMETHING IN HER EYES THAT made me think I didn't want to kill her. That certainly would have been the plan, had we had one. All I knew is that I wanted her. She had something, I saw it in her eyes, and whatever that something was, I knew I needed it in my life. She looked up at me from the trunk, and it's like, that was it. Her eyes, they weren't desperate. They were something else. Something indescribable.

That's what it was that sealed the deal. Pull the proverbial trigger—or don't— something deep inside of me usually says. It's how I choose who lives and who dies. I wish I could say it was something more elaborate, something deeper, but it isn't. It's pure gut instinct, and really, what could be more honest than that? To be honest, rarely is the answer ever in the other person's favor. With her it was different.

Maybe different was what I was looking for. It's just that after all that competing with you last year—after all of those kills, one after another—well, I guess I just got a little burned out, is all. I wanted more. I wanted something meaningful. Something lasting.

Ironically enough—that's exactly what I got. I got her, and all because things didn't go according to plan, I have her to thank. Cheryl Edwards-Steinbeck is no doubt responsible for my transformation, for bringing meaning back into my life. *Maybe that's who you were before, she said. Maybe it's not who you are now.* She's smart. It's the reason she's still around. It's that thing I see in her eyes. She sees me. And I want to see her right back.

You and I aren't in agreement on this. Even though you hide it well, it makes you angry. You'd never admit it, but from the first moment she woke up here— really woke up— there was something about it all that just made sense. Like she was something this house was missing all along, a gift that fit just right. All I know is, I'm a better person for having her here. I think there's a small part of you that sees it, too. Even if you choose to be stubborn about it. After all, it was Cheryl who gave me the idea to join the PTA; she encouraged me to get involved. It was her who thought remodeling would be a good idea. She was right about it all. I wanted to take a break from the killing, and I wanted to control the urges, and she showed me how. She said I just needed to keep myself busy, and I am. I have. Now that my days are jam packed with committee meetings, and kids, and you— I find myself far too exhausted at the end of them to think of anything but my bed. It helps that I can talk to her, tell her things, and I do. Not so much today though.

Today, I have other things on my mind. Today, I'm wrapped up in you. I have a stock of questions with your name written on them. The most pressing of all: Will you still burn for me long after the shine is gone?

∼

"KATE," YOU SAID. "THERE'S SOMETHING I WANT TO SHOW you." I guess you could say it all started with that sentence. I lived here a year before you showed me this room. A whole year, Jude, and we didn't speak of it. Not until after Olivia was born did you shove the built-in bookcase aside, take me by the hand, and let me in.

"This," you said, "is a panic room."

I looked at you sideways, anger bubbling within, quickly rising to the surface—too quickly to shove it back down the way I'd wanted to—that familiar feeling of being betrayed seeping into my pores. Back then, I couldn't have imagined something good like her could happen to this room, this house, to us.

"I hope you're not mad," you said, as you studied my profile.

Of course, I was mad! "I don't understand…" I told you once I'd almost gotten my bearings. I don't know if you saw how hard it was, or if you could tell how dry my throat had gone, how the words refused to rise as easily as my anger had.

"A person can survive in here for months," you said with a smile you shook off quickly. You read me well, and you know when you should and shouldn't act too satisfied with yourself. "But that isn't the point—it's meant to be a quick escape should you need one…"

I shifted slightly and crossed my arms. "I know what a panic room is."

You turned toward me. "Don't you want to go inside?" you asked, motioning through the door.

I sighed long and heavy. "I just don't get it."

You cocked your head, and I could see you were considering my tone. *Is this going to be a fight?* That's what you wanted to know. "I'm showing you in case you ever find yourself in trouble again…"

I shook my head. "That's not it—"

You watched my face, and you waited for me to speak. I could see that you were trying to be patient. I could also see it was taking its toll. You wanted me to show you appreciation—respect— when all I had were questions.

"What I don't understand is… how a person can live in a house and miss a whole room."

Your eyes lit up. "That's the point."

"Well, it's not *my* point."

"I thought it would make you feel safer," you said, throwing up your hands, deciding you couldn't be as patient as you'd hoped.

"Yeah, well," I told you, turning away. "You thought wrong."

~

"Coffee," she says, eyeing me as I make my way in. "I've been waiting for that."

Her eyes light up when I hand it to her, and I can tell, all that I was worried about before—her weight loss, your lies—it means nothing now. Not now that she's smiling, not now that I'm here with her. What a difference a day can make.

It's good that she's happy to see me. The coffee helps. It wasn't always this way, but thankfully we've moved past all that. It helps that she's stopped asking about him. It helps that the bitterness is gone.

Along with the coffee, I brought her flowers. It's Valentine's Day, and I want to appreciate how far we've come.

I set the coffee down, and then I slide the bag off my wrist. Once I've handed it to her I place the flowers on the bedside table. *Something is missing.*

There isn't much to the room we keep her in, which is a shame if you ask me. Turns out though, you didn't. Personally, I think we should consider adding on—a twin size bed, an armchair, with a small card table in front of it, just doesn't seem to cut it. There's another folding table, the kind old people put dinner trays on, that sits beside the bed. That's where I placed the flowers. This way she'll see them first thing when she wakes up and last thing before she drifts off.

"I love that top," she says, and it's nice when a person with so little still finds room in their heart to compliment others. Also, I like the way she always notices when something I'm wearing is new.

"That's good, seeing that I brought you one just like it," I tell her, my eyes narrowed, a smile playing on my lips. I know it sounds crazy, buying us matching clothes and all, but she doesn't seem to mind.

"Thank you," she replies, her eyes widening. She places the bag on the table and it shakes. I tell her we probably ought to replace it, get her something more fitting, more elegant, and she looks away. There used to be a lamp on top of that table— before she came. I remember how you told me it was too dangerous to keep it as we stood over her unconscious body. I watched as you yanked the cord from the wall. "Remember," you said, and there was a hint of warning in your voice. "This is only temporary."

I don't remember if I said anything. It wasn't that she and I intended for it to turn out this way, being besties and all. But how could I have known?

We argued about it yesterday. It was the first time in as long as I can remember. You'd prefer I take all the blame for this. You say I don't think things through, but you're the one who went to see her in the first place. You're the one who dragged me into the mix. I reminded you of this, although I'm not sure it helps my cause. In any case, plans change; things evolve.

I don't like being angry with you. You tell me I'm missing the point. Maybe you're right. Admittedly, I didn't see what an opportunity this could be, not immediately. But having a psychologist at the ready has really done us some good. Obviously, you would never outright say so, but having her here has become our secret weapon. She's like that magic eight ball I owned as a kid. I can ask her anything, and usually I like the answer. If not, I get to ask again the next day and the next, and it just goes on until all is right in the world. And it is—all right. I have her. Even if you're angry, even if you're second-guessing it all, deep down you know that having her here keeps me sane, keeps us on our toes. It keeps everything legit.

"You found it," she exclaims happily, removing the contents from the bag. I watch as her face lights up. It's the nail polish that she's eyeing. I like the way she says so much without saying anything at all, and she's right— it wasn't easy — but I found it. How could I not?

"What's on the agenda today?" she asks. I like this question. I like that she likes hearing about our lives.

"Well," I start, and then I pause to make sure she's listening. She always is. "The kids are having their Valentine parties today. It's so cute," I say. "They were really excited this morning... I made them cinnamon rolls, which of course

Jude said was too much. *They're already going to consume enough sugar as it is*, he said. But they're kids, you know…and he's mad at me about other stuff…so it probably wasn't even about my breakfast choice."

"I'm with you," she scoffs. "Let them be kids. It's practically a rite of childhood—" she tells me as she waves her hand in the air— "consuming too much sugar on Valentine's, that is."

"Exactly," I tell her, and it's nice that she knows so much about this stuff.

She looks away.

"Oh," I say, reaching for the bag. "Look—I brought you one."

She grins. "Had to sneak it, did you?"

"No, of course not," I lie. I don't want her to hate you. "He wants you to be happy here too, you know."

"I bet he does."

She's right, though. I did have to sneak it. You don't like it when I give her 'special treatment.' Isn't that kind of the point, I always ask. I mean, if she's going to die anyway. You don't see it that way, I guess.

"Kate?" she calls and once again my mind is on you. "Kate?"

"Sorry," I offer shaking my head—trying to get you out of it. You have that effect on me. Making me lose my mind and all. Making time stop.

"So…how is everything going?"

I jut out my bottom lip and really think about what she's asking. I shrug. "Fine, I guess."

"And the urges? How are they?"

"Manageable."

"Good," she says. "Remember what we discussed—you have to feel your feelings. If you feel sad, then feel sad. If you feel angry, be angry. But the most important thing is that you use those feelings up. Go for a run—sprint, sweat it out, if you have to. Take up boxing. Watch old, sad movies. Do anything—anything but give in."

"I will," I promise her.

She presses her lips together. "We're making great progress."

"You think?" I ask, not because I'm unsure, but because I like it when she compliments me.

"I do," she promises, and then she changes the subject. She does that a lot. I find it interesting, the way she keeps me engaged, keeps me guessing.

She lifts the cinnamon roll to her nose and inhales. It's the little things. "So—anything special going on tonight?"

"Yes," I grin. "We're having a dinner party."

"A dinner party..." she comments, and her eyes shift. Eventually she's smiling again. "I love dinner parties."

"Me, too." I tell her, although it's sort of a lie. After our fight, the last thing I want is to slap a smile on my face and pretend I'm not angry at you. "It's been awhile."

She laughs then, and I really like the sound of it. It cheers me up just a little. In that laugh, I hear everything I've missed out on my whole life by not having a friend like her. "For me, too," she says.

I sigh, because I wish she could come. Maybe someday, I think, and even as crazy as it sounds, I wonder if it might someday be a possibility. I wonder if I could make her happy enough that she'd never want to leave, and right now I think the answer is yes.

"What are you serving?"

"Roasted lamb." I answer. "I let the chef decide."

"Chef?"

I run my hands through my hair and pull it back into a ponytail "Oh, well...I mean, I think he's a chef," I tell her with a shrug. I don't want her getting too jealous. I remember her telling me how much she likes to cook. "He's just some guy Josie recommended. The food she serves always tastes great, and so I figured why not…"

"Huh."

Her one word response is infused with so much meaning that it's hard to measure. I cock my head and I wait for it. I know she has more she wants to say.

"In that case, I have this really great family recipe…I'd be happy to share it…"

"Nah," I say. "Really—he's got it covered." I laugh, but it's fake. "It's what I'm paying him for."

She leans toward the table, grabs the notepad, and jots something down. Then she hands it to me.

I stare down at the ink on the page. Tomato, red wine & chorizo risotto. I look down at her.

"Seriously, Kate. Have him make that. You won't regret it —trust me. It was my great-grandmother's recipe and I'd really love to have it again…"

I nod, and considering how thin she is, I guess it wouldn't hurt to indulge her just once. "Okay," I tell her. "I'll see what I can do."

"Thank you, again, for this," she tells me holding up the nail polish.

I wave her off. "It's nothing."

"No, it's not." She sighs. "It's not an easy color to find."

"I know. But it was always his favorite," I offer, because I want her to know that I know her, too—that I care—that I can be a good friend.

"It was," she says, and her expression shifts. Her eyes tell me she's feeling nostalgic but satisfied. I indulge her because I don't want her feeling too bad about not being on the guest list tonight. I let her talk about him for a bit. Even though it hurts my ears.

"I would love to see him again, you know," she mentions

at the end, as she most always does. By *him* one might think she's referring to her husband. She isn't. It's her lover she speaks of. "I know," I tell her.

"I hope I will. Also—I think you would really like him. It would mean so much to me if you two got the chance to meet." I don't ask her why she thinks I would like him so much. I should, but I don't. Instead, I say, "Maybe someday."

She smiles. "That's good enough for me."

It irritates me just a little to think she thinks anything could be better than what she has here, what we've built. "He was your therapist," I tell her, and there's nothing friendly in my tone. She cocks her head. "Don't you think it's a little inappropriate, what he did? Getting involved with you?"

"We were friends first. And, we were more associates than anything. He was a confidante…"

Personally, I don't see the difference. It sounds like the guy was her therapist to me, but I don't tell her this. It's probably best not to rub salt in a wound. "Why didn't it work out between the two of you? I mean—if he was so great and all…"

Her expression turns sad, even though she does her best to hide it. Her eyes can't lie as well as the rest of her face. "He had a thing for younger women."

"Hmmm," I say. "So— not that great after all…"

"It wasn't all bad. It just turned out he wasn't all that good at hiding his predications. It was terrible at the time—realizing it was never going to be anything more than what it was—that you can't make a person different." I wait for more. I like hearing that he wasn't as perfect as she's made him out to be. She shrugs and then she plasters a fake smile on her face. "But what can you do? You can't always help who you love. And sometimes you just have to let people be who they are…hindsight tends to give one a little more clarity, of course."

"You never considered murder as an option?"

She laughs. "Not really. What good would it have done? I think karma tends to have a way of working itself out."

"I get it," I say, and I leave it at that. Even though I don't get it. Not at all. But I've heard enough about him for one day. He's irrelevant. I have too much going on to be bothered by this now. Still, it's been a few days since I've seen her this happy.

It helps when we talk about him. That's why I let her go on and on.

Also, I had a breakthrough yesterday. And she really seems to like those.

"Thank you," I finally add.

"For what?"

I press my lips together. "For showing me how easy it can be to let go."

~

"THANKS AGAIN, FOR HOSTING," SCOTT SAYS, GLANCING around the table. Everything is perfect; I made sure of that. Josie helped.

"It's our pleasure," I tell him, and I smile because it is. I miss parties, and like I told her, it's been awhile.

"My wife is right," you tell the other nine people seated around our table. "It is great to have you all here. Now, let's eat."

You say this and then you look over at me. You smile, and it's you who is right. My anger subsides at your suggestion, and I know the words have more meaning than the fact that I can set a table and hire someone to throw food on it. I don't think I've ever been more in love than I am right now. "Happy Valentine's," I say, holding up my glass. You follow suit.

"Happy Valentine's," you tell me from across the table. Everyone drinks and digs in and then there's that awkward moment of silence that thankfully doesn't take long for someone to break.

"OH MY GOD, this dish is amazing, Kate," Shannon remarks. "What did you say it was called again?"

I grin. I can't help it. Cheryl was right. *She's always right.* "Tomato, red wine & chorizo risotto."

"It's not bad," Vanessa adds nonchalantly. She says it with a smile she doesn't mean.

"I'd love to snag the recipe from you," another of the women adds.

"And this dining room, the remodel—" Shannon says. "What you've done here... it's stunning."

"It just needed a fresh coat of paint, that's all."

"You did more than paint," Vanessa chimes in. She's suspicious of me, and she has a right to be.

Vanessa's husband Scott shifts in his chair. He knows his wife is being rude, and I don't know if he is simply stupid— or trying to prove a point— when he adds, "Is there anything you can't do, Kate?" His compliment is nice, I'll give him that. But he's had a few too many already, and he's trying to be charming which just makes it pathetic. He takes another sip of the good stuff. "I'm always trying to bait Jude here into dishing out at least one of his wife's flaws, but he only ever has good things to say."

"That's what happens when you marry out of your league," you offer, and you look over at Vanessa. She's frowning gloriously. You're trying to diffuse the situation and it's endearing.

"That's what happens when you're in a league of your own," I say to you, and you smile, and it lights up the room, your smile. You're happy tonight. Work is good, and business is booming. The kids are well and out of your hair. Also, aside from our argument, I've become the good wife you've always wanted. Cheryl's helping with that, of course, and she's doing a fine job. Since she's been in the picture your issues with me have been almost nonexistent. That's mostly due to the fact that keeping a captive is hard work, but also because I'm learning too much about myself to want to spend my time doing anything else.

"Don't you get sick of each other? Especially with Jude working from home so much recently?" Kelly asks dabbing the corner of her mouth with her napkin. She sticks her neck out for Vanessa's sake; she's being brave. Also, nosy. I don't answer immediately, and your eyes find mine.

"No," we both say in unison.

"I can't say we do," you add, and it's nice to see you bring your 'A game.'

"Well, I couldn't do it," Shannon says. "I need my space."

"It's not like we don't have separate interests," I reply.

"But luckily most of them are the same," you interject, and you're being coy and I like it.

"You two are crazy," Kelly comments.

"Aren't they?" Josie says, and she is beaming.

"Not crazy—" you correct her. "Just happy."

"Any advice for the rest of us?" Scott jokes even though he's two glasses of bourbon past being funny.

"Don't half-ass anything. Do it all the way," I tell him.

Everyone laughs. Everyone except Vanessa.

"And you, Jude? What do you have to say?" she asks.

"I never give advice," you say, and that's a lie.

Of course, you don't tell them that our in-house therapist is the one giving most of the advice these days. You won't admit it, not even to me, *especially* not to me, but I see it in your eyes. She's our little secret. Also, I lied, when I said I don't do anything half-ass. I do lots of things that way—just not the things I want to last.

AFTER DINNER, I'M CARRYING PLATES FROM THE DINING ROOM to the kitchen, and Vanessa, one of the newer neighbors, offers to help. I don't care for her and I don't particularly want her help. But if it helps me get these people out of our house sooner, I'm all for it, and so I accept. I just want to be alone with you. I want to feel your hands on me, and suddenly, I'm afraid I'll never get close enough. I need you now. I need to settle the disagreement we had about Cheryl.

"It must be nice," she says nostalgically. "Not to have to work."

"It is," I tell her, matching her condescending tone.

"Trouble is, I really like my job." She sighs long and slow. "It's fulfilling in a way that shuffling kids around and managing dinner parties never could be."

"That's great," I tell her. I'm determined not to let her—or anyone else— ruin my good mood. I distract myself by thinking of you inside me, and then all the stories I'm going to have for Cheryl about Vanessa, and the others. It's too bad she can't be here right now. But I shake the thought away, because even I know it's a dangerous thought.

"It is," Vanessa says, bringing me back to the here and now. "It really is amazing… I think I'll make partner soon. It's just sometimes I wish I didn't have so much ambition, you know?"

"Right," I say, which makes no sense but it's the best I can do.

"How do you do it?" she asks and that's when I know this isn't going to end well. "How do you just set it all aside? To be a *mom*, of all things. I just find it to be such an unre-warding gig."

"That's the kind of question that leads to trouble," I say, offering a sly smile. It's a warning, but she doesn't see it.

"What I mean is, how are you content with just being somebody's wife? Somebody's mom?"

"Oh," I say. "Well, I'm not just a mom. I have other interests."

"Like what?" she asks, and I give it some thought, and because murder doesn't seem like a smart thing to say, I don't say anything at all. Not at first.

Finally, it hits me. "I like to read."

"That's something," she says and then she frowns. "It wouldn't be enough for me though…I mean…I need a challenge. You know—something to strive for."

I drop the plates I'm holding directly into the sink. I don't even care how it looks, I just let them fall. Several break. I could kill her, and I want to but then I remember what Cheryl said. I just need to sweat it out. That's where you come in. In the meantime, I grip the dishtowel. I breathe in and hold it so I don't tell her to go to hell. I hold it so I don't lead her to the garage and stab her twenty-three times, once for each time she's insulted my intelligence this evening. Trouble is, my therapist-turned-friend is waiting upstairs, and I can't keep her waiting. Also, I don't want to have to explain why I couldn't manage a simple dinner party without killing someone. So, I smile, and it's almost friendly. My icy stare, not so much. "I guess we can't all be so lucky, can we?"

She tilts her head. "I guess not."

"Just remember," I say, "being the loudest person in the room does not make you the smartest."

∼

THERE'S WATER POURING FROM THE CEILING. EVERYONE stands around with their hands on their hips, at first. But not you. And certainly not me. I grab a gun. Just in case. Although obviously, I haven't thought it all the way through because I have no idea what I intend to do with it. Thankfully, you run and you shut off the water to the house. In the commotion it takes a while to notice that one of our guests has disappeared. *Scott.*

"The water," he tells you when you find him on his hands and knees staring at the bookcase. "It's coming from somewhere internal." He looks up at you. "You hear that moaning noise?"

You pretend to listen. "No," you finally say.

He leans in closer, and you clench your fists. "I'd be willing to bet you've got a leak inside these walls. That—or a pipe burst."

Kelly and Josie come around the corner, towels and sheets in hand. I take them from them and together we start mopping up the water.

"I'm not too worried," you tell him, although your face says otherwise.

"It's pretty dangerous to have a leak and let it go. Mold and all…" he says. "Anyway— know a guy…"

"No," you insist, holding your hands up. It's off-putting, abrupt, but it's you. "Thanks," you say, "but I've got it covered."

He looks back at the bookcase, shrugs and then stands. You rub at your temples. I listen for moaning, but all I hear are people rushing around trying to soak up the small flood that has overtaken our home. Our guests look weary— like this is a little more than they bargained for when they decided to get dressed up for a free dinner with people they'll only spend the rest of the evening comparing themselves to.

"My cousin is a plumber," you finally say. Another lie. I fold my lips as you take the sopping wet sheets from Josie and hand them to me. "We've got it from here," you assure them. Then you make it clear without saying so that you want everyone to go. Josie takes the hint, she always does, and she begins grabbing coats and ushering everyone out.

"Are you sure?" Scott asks, fast on your heels. "I mean, I could help, if you wanted. It'd be an easy way to save some cash…"

"No," you say again, and your tone comes out harsh. "I find it's best to leave it to the experts."

I touch the gun in the waistband of my skirt. It's too bad, I think. I feel for Scott, having to be married to an insufferable witch like Vanessa. Which is why I hope he backs off.

"Suit yourself, old boy," he sighs, placing his hand on your shoulder. "I was just trying to help."

"We're good," you promise him.

He nods and shakes your hand.

"It was a lovely evening," Shannon tells me. "I'm so sorry about the flood."

"It's not too bad," I say, and this time it's me who is the liar.

"Just let me know if you change your mind about the help," Scott says grabbing his coat. "I have a feeling I know just the thing to take care of your problem. It's a pretty simple fix."

You fold your lips, and you nod slightly, but you don't say anything in return. I'm too distracted by what's just happened to fix this for you, which is a mistake. I'm just happy I don't have to kill anyone tonight. Because if I had to choose, it wouldn't be Scott, it would be his wife. He seems like a poor second choice. Too drunk and too dense to be any fun. In any case, you think you've put it to bed for now.

But what you don't understand is that men never can turn down a good challenge.

~

"JUDE," I SIGH AFTER EVERYONE HAS GONE. "COME ON. IT wasn't her fault."

"No," you tell me. "It was yours."

"I'm sorry," I say again. "I forgot to shut off the water." I offer my apology again because the first five times seem to have flown right over your head.

"She flooded our house, Kate."

"It was an accident…"

"When we had a house full of guests?" you say, running your fingers through your hair. "Seriously? You want me to buy that?"

"I don't want you to buy anything. I'm telling you she wouldn't do such a thing on purpose. She's happy here."

You rub your hand over your face, and then pinch the bridge of your nose. "Answer me this Kate—did you or did you not tell her we were having company?"

"I didn't," I say and I must be convincing because you let it go.

It's the first time I've lied to you in a long time.

It won't be the last.

～

"I'M A NOBODY," I TELL HER WHEN I TAKE IN A GLASS OF WATER seeing that she'll have none for a while. I bring her a glass of red, also, but not any of her grandmother's dish. I'm slightly past that kind of generosity. I'm probably not going to get laid tonight, unless you're up for a revenge fuck, and all the water downstairs tells me that's a pipe dream.

She doesn't know it yet but her wine is spiked. I need her to sleep for a day, maybe two. The water damage guys are coming, you're pissed, and right now we don't need any further distractions.

"You're in a mood," she notes, gulping the wine.

"No," I tell her my voice full of melancholy. "Just another suburban housewife in a vast sea of them who will be long forgotten. No one will care about my special recipe or the fact that—best case scenario—I turned out two relatively well adjusted children," I add and I sigh. "And even that much is up in the air at this point…"

"Wow," she says raising her brow. "That bad huh?"

"All that work we did on the remodel—all of it—has gone to shit."

"That is bad," she says. "But don't worry— insurance should cover it."

"Yeah."

"Have you called them yet?"

I look up at her and cock my head. "Jude seems to think you had something to do with this," I say. I shake my head slightly, "But I know better. I mean… you know the dining room is just below. And you and I put so much work into making it what it was…I just can't see…"

"I remember," she interrupts. Her tone is light, cheery. "You had me pouring over design and decorating magazines for months. We did it together. And look how it turned out."

"Yes," I say. "Which is why I keep telling Jude he's wrong."

She studies my face.

"But he isn't wrong is he, Cheryl?" I make a tisking sound, and she cocks her head. "I don't understand," I say to her as I stand. I shake my head again, wishing it weren't so. "I thought you were happy here."

"I am happy," she tells me. But she's lying.

"Tonight was supposed to be good for us. For all of us. Now look what you've done…"

"I'm sorr—" she starts to say, but it's too late. I'm already pressing the taser to her neck.

≈

CHAPTER THREE

JUDE

The alarm goes off at 5:00 a.m. on the dot. I'm not asleep when it comes blaring to life, and I'm hoping if I let it go on for a bit, you won't be either. We need to talk. I look over, but you're unfazed. I shift and lay one arm across you, before pulling you in tight. You snuggle into me, it's automatic, you're sleeping contently, blissfully unaware of all that needs to get done. I, on the other hand, find it a bit more difficult to ignore reality.

I run down this list in my mind of what has to get done today, and I haven't a clue how I'll fit it all in. Eventually, I come up with a loose plan. Having a strategy in place and the curve of your hip against my body, seem to do the trick, by the time I climb out of bed, I'm slightly less agitated. I don't do much without really thinking it through. Except when it comes to you. I hadn't foreseen that killing one man was going to complicate my life this much. Nevertheless, it did, mostly because it wasn't a part of the plan and so the work keeps rolling in. More and more every day, of what was his, is becoming mine. Turns out, thanks to you and your poor decision-making, his wife included.

From the beginning, I told you she wasn't staying, that this was a temporary solution to a temporary problem. I told you we couldn't keep her—but you don't seem to care what I have to say. You like her here. You're right about what you said last night. I didn't mind so much at first, not when I thought you might still have a bit of reason left in you. Then you started buying her clothes, and books—and nail polish, for God's sake— and it became clear, you don't reason well. You act like she's a special houseguest—not someone we agreed to murder. You say it's making us better, having her here. I think you want a pet, a project, something to keep you entertained. More than anything, I think you just want someone to agree with you. I thought I could handle it, and I have. But I've let it go on for long enough.

It's time to kill her, Kate. I know it and you know it, even if you won't admit it. It's time to get on with our lives. And that is exactly why I'm up an hour earlier this morning.

∽

I'M STARING OUT THE KITCHEN WINDOW WAITING FOR THE coffee to finish brewing and before I know it I'm nine years old again and back in my childhood home. "Oh, stop, Jude," my mother says peering at me over her gin and tonic. "Is getting up an hour earlier really such a big deal?"

I don't say anything. It's best not to indulge her when she's had a few.

"I mean… come onnnnn," she insists drawing out her words. She waves her hands in the air and I watch as the contents of her glass swish and sway, spilling over the rim and on to the floor. "There are starving children in Africa, and you're mad because you have to give up your bedroom for a few weeks."

"I'm not mad," I tell her, staring at the puddle on the tile.

She scowls. "You just want your beauty rest, I get it."

I watch as she floats across the kitchen. She stops short of the counter and reaches for the bottle of gin. I've diluted it with water, which I hope helps as she refills her glass. For the third time. That I've seen.

"No one told you that you had to wake up any earlier—that's on you."

"I don't want to be here when she gets up…"

She places her drink on the counter hard, pinches the bridge of her nose and then closes her eyes. It seems like forever before she opens them again. She looks over at me, she's gotten her second wind. "You and your father, I swear! You don't want me to be happy."

"We don't even know her—"

"What's to know?" she demands, throwing up her hands. "She's a girl down on her luck. She just needs a place to stay…"

"Did it have to be my bedroom?" I ask. The words slip out nice and easy. I regret them as soon as they're out. I know it's best not to argue with her when she's like this, but I'm damned if I do, damned if I don't. My father warned me last time, after she nearly burned the house down. He told me I have to watch out for her. More importantly, he said I have to learn to stand up to her. I wanted to tell him it doesn't seem to be working out so well for him. But I thought better of it.

"Did it have to be your bedroom?" she slurs, shaking her head from side to side. "Did it have to be *your* bedroom?" she repeats lifting her tumbler from the counter to her lips. She glares at me over the rim. "You ungrateful little shit."

"It's just—"

"It's just nothing. It's just you don't like sharing me. You don't want me having any friends. You think I don't know

41

what you're up to…" she tells me downing what's left in her glass. She sets it down and lifts the bottle.

"No, mom," I say taking the bottle from her hand. She rears back. "That's enough," I tell her, not taking my eyes from hers. "No more." Last time, I had to drag her to the toilet and help her in ways that no kid my age should ever have to help their mom. This is why I can't have friends. I'd have to make up stuff to talk about and I'd certainly never be able to invite them over.

"This is my house, I'm an adult, and I can do as I damned well please," she seethes, doing her best to take the bottle back and suddenly we're playing hot potato, bouncing around the kitchen, only there's nothing funny nor enjoyable about this version of the game. I move quickly to the left, she goes right, and as she does I watch in slow motion as she wipes out on the liquor she spilled. Her feet fly out from under her, and she goes down hard. I watch, helplessly, placing one foot in front of the other. I try to get to her, I try to make a catch I know defies the laws of physics. The back of her head clips the corner of the bar.

I can't catch my breath. My mother whimpers, but she isn't dead, and she isn't unconscious. Meanwhile my heart feels like it's going to burst out of my chest and slide across the kitchen floor. I grab my mom's purse from the counter, run to my bedroom and bang on the door. When the girl opens it I hold out my mom's keys and tell her we need a ride to the E.R. She stares at me for a long time without saying anything. "I don't do hospitals," she says finally, without taking her eyes from mine. She leans back against the door jamb, crosses her arms, her mouth slack with defiance. Already, I know this look. I know what it means. It's a test. I see it in my mother everyday.

"My mom gave you a place to stay when you had no where to go…the least you—"

She shrugs and cuts me off. "And?"

"And— you're driving us to the hospital."

"Your mother is a drunk. She needs help."

I don't say anything. I simply grab her wrist and pull in the direction of the front door.

"Why don't you just call an ambulance?" the girl demands standing over my mom. She's been staying in my room for a week—my mother found her at the local bar— by now she should know why I'm not calling for help. I glance over at her, and wonder why she would ask such a stupid question at a time like this, but it makes sense in a way, she sure doesn't look like a grown-up.

"They'll take me away."

"Yeah," she says eyeing me up and down, sizing me up. "Probably."

"I'm not that good at driving," she tells me, as she fumbles with the key in the ignition. Her voice is laden with uncertainty I'm too young to understand.

I chew on my bottom lip and consider what a disaster this is, and how my dad is going to kill me if I let this girl crash our car. "Can you get us there or not?"

She looks over her shoulder at me holding a towel to the back of my mother's head. My mother speaks inaudibly; she's slumped over in the seat. The girl twists her mouth. "I can get you there."

I nod.

She eyes me in the rearview mirror. "But I'm not going in."

I don't say anything. I know it's better that way.

"You see," my mother says, raising her voice, flinging her arms. Her breath smells of liquor and sickness, and I want to get as far away as I can, but when she asks I let her rest her head on my lap. "This is why we need her around."

"Yes," I say, shushing her. I read in one of my survival

books that when a person is injured it's best to keep them calm. "You're right, mom," I tell her. It's a lie. Sometimes they're necessary in situations like these. Sometimes you have to tell a person they're not going to die even if you know they are. Not that my mom is going to die now. But if she keeps this up, it's inevitable. I stare out the window; it's better than looking at the blood seeping through the towel onto my jeans. I stare at the sun, even though they say you aren't supposed to. It's just coming up, and it looks promising, even if nothing else around me does. I rub at my eyes. None of us slept through the night, and I know sleep is still so far off. I remember that hospitals take a long time and they ask a lot of questions. I remember from the last time, when she fell in the shower. I close my eyes, but I'm too tired to sleep. It's always like this when my father is away. I make a silent vow, that if I ever have kids, they'll never have to worry.

In the end, my mother got twelve stitches and a brochure for AA. We never did see that car again. Or most of the items that were worth anything in our house. My father didn't speak to me for a full month, my mother only when she had to.

～

IT's CALLED THE TRICKLE DOWN EFFECT. THAT's WHAT's happening here. Something seemingly insignificant happens, and it affects everything. In this case, we 'accidentally' kidnapped a man's wife, and then I had to kill said man in order to keep him from A) finding out the truth and B) killing me and/or my entire family. That's how this business works. *An eye for an eye.*

It's not that I minded putting a bullet in his head. Not one bit. It wasn't exactly a concession. I never much cared for him anyway. The problem lies in the fact that I have a constant reminder of him, trapped in a room in my house. That's not smart business, Kate. Even you have to admit that. Sooner or later, something has to give, and what we're waiting for, I'm not sure.

"It's all going to be fine," you like to say. "Don't worry so much," you told me last night. But it isn't fine, and I am worried.

If someone finds out about her, we're goners. Not to mention the fact that we have children. What if they find her? What if she finds them? I learned the hard way, taking in strangers never leads anywhere good.

In this case, it's even worse. Eventually people will start asking questions. Lies tend not to stay lies forever. Tell enough of them and eventually it catches up with you. But you know who can't tell lies? Dead people, that's who.

Speaking of dead people, when a hitman disappears not many people question it. It's sort of par for the course in this line of work. When the shit hits the fan, you have to cut and run, you have to become someone new, somewhere else. That's what people think her husband did. And he is somewhere else, all right. He's dead in the water.

But she isn't—and if you weren't already aware, that makes her a liability. Which is why his better half, for whom I've just made toast and coffee, (two sugars, no cream, just the way you say she likes it) should have joined him in his resting place by now. In fact, she would have, if it weren't for you. I'm not going to live out the rest of my life in a cold, dark cell because of your impulsiveness. Don't worry, I want to say to you now. It's all going to be fine. Not because you tell me so, but because I intend to make it that way.

≈

I TYPE IN THE CODE, AND THE DOOR OPENS. I CAN SEE ON THE monitor above the door that she's still asleep. She isn't expecting anyone this early. It's important to change things up, you would do well to keep that in mind.

She doesn't stir as I enter. I set the tray with the toast and coffee down beside her, the syringe full of liquid I plan to use to stop her heart, tucked neatly into the pocket of my jeans.

She doesn't open her eyes; she pretends to sleep, when she and I both know she's playing possum. I haven't got time for such games. Which is why it's been a while since I've been in. After all, she's your pet, not mine.

"Good morning," I say and she doesn't look up. I set the tray down hard, it causes the table to shake. We should probably replace it, but why bother. She doesn't flinch, doesn't bat an eye at my presence, doesn't fight to get away. She never has, and that's one of the things I find most odd about this whole situation. It's like she likes being here. I think she enjoys being the victim for a change. It suits her.

"Is it?" she finally answers quietly. She doesn't open her eyes but there's venom in her voice. Go figure.

"Well, I think so," I say. I study her carefully. She's thin— she isn't the same woman we abducted on that bright, sunny, too hot afternoon months ago. Time has changed her, at least so far as her appearance goes, and I have to admit, I'm shocked. "You would think that," she tells me with a slur. "Your crazy ass wife tasered me last night. So— forgive me if I'm not exactly pleased to see you."

"You flooded the downstairs of our home. While we had guests in the house. A tasing seems like a small price to pay if you ask me…"

"You know," she whispers. Her voice is rough, like a smokers. It didn't used to be that way. "You may find this surprising but—I've been ready for this from day one."

I don't say anything in return. I give her space. She wants

to demand more, she wants me to take her bait, there's something she wants me to know, but I won't beg for it. Women will always tell you the rest of whatever it is they have to say, just give them time.

"It's Kate, though," she confesses and she lets out a long sigh. Eventually she picks up where she left off but it takes her some time, and I can't help but wonder if she's closer to death than I thought. "It's your wife who isn't ready, I'm afraid."

"Right," I say, and I finger the syringe.

"And it's you—I'm certain—who doesn't realize how much of a problem that's going to be."

"How so?" I ask even though I have a vague idea. I almost choke on the words as I say them, mostly because it bothers me that I care to hear the answer.

She doesn't open her eyes, but her chin quivers, and I can tell this isn't easy. "Much as I hate it—I'm helping her."

"She doesn't need your help."

She seems to consider what I've said for a few moments before she opens her eyes and looks up. She blinks several times. "Let me ask you a question—"

I stare at her, my expression blank.

She continues. "Does she even know you're here?"

I squat down to her level. But I don't answer, and that's how she knows to take aim.

"You haven't a clue what Kate needs," she tells me weakly. "And that's your first mistake," she adds, licking her lips. "I don't get it—I don't get you at all." She shakes her head. "I thought I had you figured out. My mistake, I guess." She pauses to half-laugh. "Now, I realize maybe you're just as crazy as she is—which is sad, if you ask me. You're the one who stands to lose the most—along with those children," she says, and she tries to sit up a little. "You see, Jude—it really doesn't matter whether I'm dead or alive, not to me. Not

47

anymore… But I would suggest—before making that call—that you make sure you have a contingency plan in place—at least for your kids— if nothing else."

"Of course," I agree. But it's clear, I'm caught off guard by her assessment of me, not to mention how much she seems to know about you, about our life. Although, I guess I shouldn't be.

She swallows, and I can see she's in a bit of pain. "Unless, of course, you already do."

I stand, and I dust myself off. She's called my bluff, and I want to kill her all the more for it. "Let's be clear—" I say to her. "If I wanted you dead—you would be."

She doesn't respond. She doesn't have to. She's already done her damage.

"It just so happens that I have several other matters on my plate at the moment. With your husband tied up, business is booming," I say and I leave it to her to infer what she will. She's a smart woman and for the first time all morning I'm thankful for that.

She still doesn't answer. She won't let me get to her that easily.

I make a start for my exit. She steadies her gaze on me. "It's too bad that you're ready to die—you know—that you're just willing to give up— to let yourself waste away. Because the truth of it is— you keep Kate nice and distracted—and out of the way. You think you know me… but you're wrong. Because if you did, then you'd know you're worth more to me alive."

The words she utters next are so faint I wonder if I'm hearing her right at all. "It's nice that we have an understanding, you and me. According to your wife… you can be quite hard to deal with." I stand with my hands on my hips at the door, and I consider my next move. It hardly seems satisfying to kill her now. Finally, she tells me. "It's refreshing to see that she's not right all of the time."

∾

WHEN I LEAVE HER, I FIND YOU IN THE SHOWER. IT PUZZLES ME that when you wake, and you don't find me in the bed next to you, that you don't assume that I've gone to kill her. That's the problem, Kate. You're too trusting.

I step into the bathroom and close the door. The kids will be up soon, which means I have to make this quick. I shed my clothes and along with them the unease of my encounter with your pet, and I join you, letting the hot water wash away my bad intentions.

"Good morning," you say. I swear it's like déjà vu.

"Is it?" I ask, quirking my brow.

You grin. It turns you on when I'm in a bad mood because you aren't normal. "It is now," you murmur. When you begin lathering soap onto my chest, I don't reply, I don't say anything. I lose all train of thought. It's like tunnel vision where all I see is your hands working their magic.

You aren't going to get me this easy though. No matter how good you look naked. "I don't like having her here with the kids, or the workers, or the insurance people," I tell you with a huff. Partly, because I'm frustrated, and partly because of what you're doing to me.

You pause, your hands still against my chest. You're annoyed, I can tell by the way you bite your lip. I, too, realize what bad timing this conversation is but I can't help myself.

I take a step backward. You let your hands drop.

You step forward. "She's been here for months, Jude."

"That's my point. Every day, the risk goes up."

"Relax," you say, closing any distance there was between

us, putting your hands on me again, this time gently, moving them lower, inch by inch. "No one is finding anybody."

"Where does this end, Kate?" I demand and I know I should just shut my mouth and let you do what you do best, but I can't. I won't.

"We just need a plan," you say, stroking me. "And you— well, you just need to relax and let me handle it."

I watch your eyes shift, and then I do let you handle it. You slip me inside of you, and I do relax. You're wet and soapy and so sure of yourself. Suddenly, it looks like we have a plan, and it's one you're very good at.

Which, as it turns out, is why I'm in the position I'm in. Back against the wall and all.

~

AFTERWARD, AS I DRY YOUR BACK, IT'S YOU WHO BRINGS UP OUR 'situation.'

"I bet she's wondering where I'm at this morning," you sigh. "She's probably going crazy waiting for her coffee," you tell me and no one in particular, because I don't care. You're talking fast, excitedly and that's about to change. "It's so cold in that room..."

"I took her coffee."

You deadpan.

I'm not one to beat around the bush. "She thinks she's helping you, Kate."

You swallow and I can see you're not sure where I'm going with this. "She is," you finally say.

I look away. It's always when you think I'm not looking that you let me in. "The voices— I haven't heard them since she's been here—and the nightmares have all but stopped." I look back at you. "She listens, Jude. She's a therapist— it's what she's trained to do. Help people..."

"I see," I tell you, even though I don't see at all.

"It's not forever—" you promise, and I've heard that one before. "Just until I make sure we have things under control. I mean… look at us." You pause, fold your lips and eye me in the mirror. You're begging me to disagree with you. "Look how happy we are. Even the neighbors saw it."

I purse my lips, and I have to get to work, so I won't argue. Not now. You're right, it isn't forever. I don't know what the answer is, only that I don't need you unstable, not right now. Not with so much at stake. Not with me working so much. She has something you want—I just can't figure out what that something is.

Mostly because she's a dreadful woman, Kate. Nothing at all like you. On the flip side, if that's what you want to be, then I give up. We can call it quits right here. You are soft and crazy and lovely. That woman—she is cold and calculating and hard to the core. She is playing you, and there's nothing lovely about being played. But if I know you, then I know you're destined to find this out the hard way.

And even though in the afterglow of sex, I may concede temporarily, that is what I'm afraid of more than anything.

～

CHAPTER FOUR

KATE

I'm poring over Pinterest, looking at flooring and saving off photos I can run by Cheryl just as soon as she learns her lesson, when the phone rings. I'm running late for a committee meeting for the Spring Carnival at the kids' school, and now there's this to deal with. Repairs and insurance people and a captive I'm refusing to speak to.

She needs a few days to think about what she's done. To remind her how good I've been to her, to see what she's missing out on. Ever since the flood incident, the phone hasn't stopped ringing, it's all contractors, repairmen and our insurance agent. Quite frankly, I'm tired of talking to people. I decide to let it go to voicemail but then it starts again. This time, I check the number on the screen. It's the school, and I'm guessing it isn't about the carnival, although a part of me hopes. I press the button, and my heart sinks. I know what this call means. Someone has gone to the nurse with a fever, someone needs a change of clothes, someone has lost their lunch. Either literally or figuratively.

"Hello."

"May I speak to Mrs. Riley?"

"This is she."

"Mrs. Riley, this is Meg Quinlen. I'm the principal here at Hilltop Academy."

I know who she is. I guess the introduction is customary. "Yes," I say.

She inhales into the phone. "I'm afraid there's been an incident with Brady."

My breath catches, and she can hear it. School officials are pretty good about knowing these things and so she moves to ease my mind. "He's fine. He's in my assistant's office now, in fact."

I exhale loudly. My hand goes to my chest.

"I am however, going to ask that you come and pick him up for the day," she informs me, like it's no big deal. "We're still in the process of gathering facts— but it appears that Brady may have pushed another child off the playscape."

"That doesn't sound like Brady," I tell her. Sure, he has a history of pushing. But I don't offer this info up. Anyway, it's been awhile.

"Well, the other child has been taken to the hospital…. With a broken arm and a possible concussion…."

"Oh."

"Brady insists it was an accident. But some of the other kids say that the injured child and Brady had some sort of dispute."

"A dispute?" I ask, because I can't think of anything else reasonable to say.

"Basically, your son isn't talking, Mrs. Riley. We're aware of his issues and feel the best course of action is to suspend him for a day or two until we can gather all the facts."

I scoff. "We pay a lot of money to send our kids to your school. And I'm not sure what issues you're referring to, Ms. Quinlen, but I'm pretty sure my child has the same right to an education that everyone else does. "

"Not when he is endangering other students."

"You said yourself you don't have all the facts."

I hear her exhale, long and slow. "Look—Mrs. Riley. The fact is, I have parents breathing down my neck. When a child is injured on our campus, we take it very seriously. It's my responsibility to do due diligence here. Therefore, we have no choice but to suspend Brady."

"And, if Brady has done nothing wrong—which you can't in fact prove that he has—what then?"

"Then you will have a full apology. But if he isn't talking, and if he doesn't plan to, well, then it makes it difficult to prove anything."

I smile then. I can't help myself. Brady may have gotten himself in trouble. But he knows when to shut his mouth. That kid is very, very smart.

∼

"Mommy," Olivia tells me as we're driving home from dance lessons. "Why did Brady get to come home early and I didn't?"

"The school said Brady pushed someone. They want him to stay home while they work it out."

"Yeah…" she says. "I saw. Matthew's bone was sticking out. It was kinda cool. "

"You saw?" I ask doing a double take. It hadn't occurred to me that her class might have been on the playground, too.

"There wasn't any blood. Not like in the movies."

"When did you see blood in movies?"

"With Daddy."

"Of course."

"But his arm!" she says and her face lights up. "His arm was just hanging there."

"Hmm."

"Why would your brother push him?" I ask, because I can already see that she knows the answer.

"He was calling him 'mute-boy.'"

"Mute boy?"

"He got his friends to do it, too," she tells me, her little brow furrowed.

"And then what?"

"And then, Brady waited until Matthew was at the top of the slide and he just ran at him. Matthew went over the side…and down…down…down until—"

"Why didn't you say anything?" I ask, cutting her off.

"I didn't want Brady to get in trouble."

"No, Liv. I mean about those boys calling him names."

She shakes her head slightly and juts out her bottom lip. Her face is set, and it's determined, which is how I know I won't like what comes next. "I took care of it on my own. Like Daddy told me to."

"You what?"

"Matthew. He's allergic."

"Allergic?"

"Yeah—" she tells me and her eyes light up. I'm forced to look back at the road. "So I snuck one of my Girl Scout cookies in his lunch box. The kind with nuts."

"Oh my God." It hits me hard, right in the gut, what really happened.

"I told Brady he wouldn't be bothering him anymore," she says, and I swear she sounds just like you.

"So Brady pushed him."

I glance in the rearview and she looks confused.

"Olivia, that cookie could've killed Matthew…"

"But he isn't nice, though. Daddy says sometimes bad people have to die."

"Oh, Liv. Daddy didn't mean kids…"

She shrugs, and a lump forms in my throat. I hold my

breath the entire way home, and I don't let it out, not really, not until I've spoken to Cheryl. I can't be mad at her, not at a time like this. She always knows exactly the right thing to say.

⌁

WE'RE SITTING ON THE COUCH ADJACENT TO ONE ANOTHER, MY feet resting on your lap. You take my big toe in your hand, and you squeeze. You don't like just sitting, but you are, mostly because you're placating me. You have a full day ahead of you, and I'm pretend pouting that you have to go.

"Let's get one thing clear," you tell me, and your face is serious. You lower your voice because Brady is home again today. "I did not tell her to hurt anyone specifically. I simply told her that sometimes you have to take matters into your own hands—that's all."

"Jude—that kid could've died because of that kind of advice. I can't believe I'm the one telling *you* this…but it's reckless."

"It depends on the context," you say, and you never can admit when you're wrong. "Anyway, we spoke about it, and I think we're clear now."

"You think. Well, that's reassuring."

"He can't let kids go around picking on him his whole life, Kate. And they will, if he allows it."

"What are you suggesting? That our kids team up and take them all out?"

You check your watch. "I have to run."

"Wait," I say. "I need to talk to you about something…"

"Can it wait? I'm going to be late if I don't head out now."

"Brady pushed that kid because he knew Olivia had given him those cookies. He might've saved his life."

"Yes…"

"And yet, he's the one in trouble. It's not fair."

"Life isn't fair."

"He's protecting his sister."

"That's what family does."

I sigh, long and heavy. I don't have the energy to go hand-to-hand with you. "I'm tired," I tell you. "And that woman is right about me," I add. It's a confession, which you obviously take as a complaint. I can tell by the way you squeeze my foot harder. It hurts. "Like I told Cher—" I start and not only do you squeeze harder, this time you twist. You don't want to talk about her, but also because you hate it when I call her that. It's a warning, a cheap shot.

"Her name is Cheryl."

I try to pull my foot away, but I can't. Your grip is unforgiving. Like you.

"It's a nickname."

"We don't do nicknames in this house," you say, but it's a lie. You call our daughter Olive, for God's sake.

I glance at the clock. "Whatever—anyway. Like I told her…all I do is shuffle kids around…. I don't have a purpose anymore. It's all kids and you and a long list of to-dos… and then I wake up and do it all over again the next day. It's like fucking *Groundhog Day* around here. I miss the thrill of…"

"You need to stop going to see her for a while. Put a bit of space between the two of you."

"What?"

"You've gotten too close, Kate. Take a step back. Get some perspective."

"What has that got to do with anything?"

"You're saying you have too much on your plate…"

"So?"

"So—stop going in for a few days. If you need less to worry about, start there. She has enough food and water to last her."

I twist my wedding rings. "I think you're wrong."

"Shocker," you reply. Your jaw twitches and it doesn't go unnoticed.

"You're wrong about her. I don't need space. I need to discuss the situation with Brady with her."

You tilt your head and give me the look that lets me know you think I'm crazy.

I set you straight. "She'll know what to do. She's a psychologist. This is what she's trained to do…"

"We're his parents."

"Maybe that's the problem," I say.

"Maybe you need to listen to me for once, Kate. Would it kill you to consider that maybe I know what I'm talking about?"

"Maybe—It sounds like you're asking me to choose. I don't think that's a good idea…"

"Surely, you're not suggesting that you'd choose a stranger over your own husband."

I frown. It's like you don't understand me at all. "She's not a stranger."

"Through no fault of your own."

"I don't know what you want me to say…"

You move my legs off you, and you start to stand. "It isn't that."

"Jude…I'm not finished."

"This conversation is a road to nowhere," you tell me, gathering your things. I watch you pick up my set of keys, put them down, and search for yours. "Just consider what I said. Stop being so obsessed with her. Surely, even *you* can see she's playing you."

"If anything, she's helping."

"Right," you say, and you kiss my cheek. "Stay away, Kate," you warn and then you walk away. When you get to the door you pause, looking back over your shoulder. "You'll be better for it."

I press my lips together, and that's when I see that thing in your eyes, the thing that nearly does me in. Sometimes with you it's not much, a glance in my direction, a nod, the sound of your voice saying hello. Other times it's everything, it's your fist reaching in, taking hold of my heart, controlling its rhythm, giving me life and taking it with you when you go.

~

Stay away, Kate. You'll be better for it. The words ring in my ears. I've heard them before. I shake my head doing my best to will the memory away. But it pulls me in, swirling back and forth, bouncing around inside my head. It's like water circling the drain, those words. They are sucking me in, taking me down with them.

"Please don't go Father," I plead. "You don't have to do this… I'll be better, I promise."

It takes everything in me not to call him Daddy. It still happens, sometimes, especially when I'm scared. Habits are hard to change, he says that, and it's what I've called him since I learned to talk. All these years later and suddenly everything is different. I'm not Daddy's little girl any longer, and he isn't the dad I once knew. I bite my tongue quite literally just to avoid saying the words. That's the funny thing about words, it feels like I'm forever trying to keep them in, or get them out. Once again, he insists that I refer to him only as *father* and so I make an effort. I don't want to face the punishment, not again. But it seems no matter what I do, I can't win. His wrath is inevitable. Business is down, I know because I heard him yelling at my mother, and I know what happens when business is bad.

I swallow the familiar taste of blood.

"I told you," he says. "You aren't to see that girl. You never listen...would it kill you, for once, just to listen to what I tell you to do?"

"I'm sorry—"

"You're such a disappointment," he tells me again, this time as he attaches the all too familiar shackles. "You know how much I hate doing this Lyd— I don't know why you have to make me. You've gone soft, that's what's happening here. You're possessed. That girl is the devil in the flesh, and she's winning, Lydia. You're choosing her over this family and it has to be stopped. You're ruining yourself, you're ruining my good name." I don't tell him that his good name was ruined long ago, back when he first became friends with the bottle, back when business first began to go bad. He lowers his voice and clasps the metal against my wrist. "She's lured you in, and no child of mine will be lured by the devil. I'll be damned—"

"I'm not lured Dadd—"

"Oh, child. Bless you," he says, signing the cross. When business is bad, he turns to God. God and whiskey.

"I am blessed Father," I tell him this because sometimes he likes these words, sometimes they work.

"I am your Father, and you shalt obey me," he tells me, and I realize then it's too late. He's too far gone. Any pleas I have left in me will only fall on deaf ears. If he mentions the word obey or starts quoting the bible, that's the end of it.

Still, I'd do almost anything to avoid what I know is coming. I consider my options. There aren't many. I watch as he places a diagonal line on the chalkboard. "That's one mark for you."

I feel the tears sting my eyelids and even though I don't want to, I cry because there's no turning back now. I know how he gets when he has that look in his eye, when his breath reeks of alcohol. I know what comes next.

"You will sit here and study this line, and while you suffer you will know that your suffering is not for nothing. It's to make you whole again. It's for the line you crossed."

He takes a step back and places his head in his hands. "You will suffer, but by God, you will learn. You will know hunger the same way you know sin."

When I don't answer, he looks up. "Do you understand what this means?"

"Yes, Father," I say because at this point it's helpful to be agreeable. Sometimes he forgets when he sobers up. For now, it is what it is. Also, it's best not to provoke him when he's this angry.

"State your sins, child," he demands.

"I went to see her."

He crosses his arms and looks pleased. More with himself than with me. He nods his head up and down and taps his foot. If only he were close to passing out. He isn't. He's in the manic phase of his drunkenness. I read about it in a book. I learned the signs. Sometimes it helps to know. Mostly, it doesn't.

"And when did you commit your sin, child?"

"After school," I say. I'm no child, not anymore. I leave that part out.

He grabs the bottle from his stool, twists the cap, and throws his head back. If I could keep him talking, it might get me closer to the point where he gives up. It might get worse, too. Things could go either way, and after last time, I'm not sure I'm willing to gamble with my fate that way.

He swallows and places the cap back on the bottle. "Now —what do you have to say for yourself?"

"I know better."

"Exactly. She is the devil. I want to hear you say you went to see the devil."

"I can't say that, Daddy. She's my friend," I tell him and the words slip out smooth and easy, like they don't give a damn.

He steps forward and slaps me. Hard. "You're too soft, Lydia. You don't have what it takes, and I won't have a daughter like you. I won't. Where you are weak, I will make you strong…"

When I hear the familiar sound of his belt buckle loosening, I know then, I should have just said what he wanted me to say.

I didn't, and it's too late. He's too far gone to let me take it back now.

Next time I choose a different route.

This time, I stayed in the dark without food for three days. Beaten and bloodied. All because, in theory, he was right, I'd gone soft. All because I desperately wanted a friend.

≈

CHAPTER FIVE

JUDE

You don't know it yet, but we have a date. It's been a while, thanks to our houseguest. Even before her, though. After all, it's hard to find a good sitter to begin with. Throw in the fact that you're holding a woman hostage in the belly of your house, and well, it can feel downright impossible.

Still, you need this. You've been down over everything with the kids, and I know you have a lot on your plate. I figure a night away will do you good. To commence the special occasion, I intend to surprise you with a dress. A dress that reminds you that you aren't just someone's mom. You're beautiful and clever and you just need a reminder, that's all. I don't know for sure, but I assume this is the kind of thing women like. With you, it's hard to tell; it depends on the day.

We need to get back to the way things were *before.* Before she came. Before all of this with her began. You're getting too close, and she isn't helping, not the way you think. I'm hoping tonight will help you see; you don't need her.

There's only one problem with the little surprise I have in

mind. I don't particularly like shopping, which is why I go to one of those department stores that has personal shoppers. Personally, I don't understand the concept. The very idea of needing approval so much that you'd pay someone to do your bidding for you, all the way down to the clothing you wear, strikes me as needy, pretentious, and disgusting, but what can I say? I'm a man. You don't have to hire a personal shopper, not because you're not pretentious, but because you're lucky. You have me.

When I finally find the right dress department—who knew there could be so many? I quickly realize this little excursion isn't going to be as easy as I originally thought. For starters, the woman working the floor is talking two octaves higher than what's actually required to get the job done, which makes it obvious she's the kind of woman who wants to be heard. I almost leave. But I'm not a quitter. I just hope you appreciate the effort I'm going to. This shopping thing isn't easy. It's absolutely dreadful. I don't immediately see who the woman is talking to, all I know is that it should be me, so that I can get the hell out of here. Apparently, it's someone in the fitting room, and she thinks that justifies the rest of us needing to hear the entirety of her conversation.

I take a deep breath in and let it out. I can do this. I'm not even in a bad mood today. In fact, I'm happy. I'm happy I get to be with you. I'm happy about our night away. I'm happy about the business we have to attend to, and most of all, I'm happy that it'll be just like old times.

"It's perfect. Just go with it…you'll see," the worker calls out. You tell me later that calling her a 'worker' is offensive, but that's what she is. I shut my eyes, trying to tune the woman out. Her voice is grating, and it doesn't help that she's making me wait, even though I already know what I want to buy. She does it on purpose, I know. She does it so that I'll purchase more than I came for, but I'm not stupid. I'm a man, and men don't fall for that kind of bullshit. I feel my blood pressure rising by the second, and so I loosen my tie, adjust my collar. She takes notice, and she smiles, but it doesn't touch her eyes. She doesn't care; she doesn't have passion for her job, and it's obvious. Quite frankly, I don't care either. I just want a damned dress, and if I have to help myself, then so be it. Her laziness and her inability to multitask is keeping me from you, from the rest of my life, and that is what bothers me most.

I'm about to make my move when she turns. I stand at the counter, eyeballing her, and it doesn't hit me right then what bothers me most about this woman, but later I'll realize it's because she sounds like my mother. For now, I'm ready to go, to get on with it, all the while she mostly ignores me and pretends to focus on hanging clothes. I clear my throat. It does nothing to sway her. This woman, I don't know what her deal is, but she's intent on making me wait. Also, there's something in her nonchalance that reminds me a bit of you. But then she turns around and that all changes. Head on, and up close, her features are striking—off-putting—just like her voice, and her face isn't friendly, not at all. This time, when she looks at me, she wears one of those expressions, the kind people have when they're permanently pissed off. You say it's the kind I have, too, but I think you confuse pissed off with intense.

A woman emerges from the dressing room, an older woman of about sixty, and the attendant turns away again. The older woman holds a dress, and I can tell by her expression that she isn't sold; she hasn't found what she's come for, and judging by the quality of the help, I can't say I'm surprised. She hands the attendant the items and shakes her head. "I tried, I did," she says looking iffy, if not all together displeased. "I just don't think these are my style," she adds, looking at the dresses the worker has begun hastily returning to their rightful places. "People never listen..." the attendant chides. She looks at me. "What can you do?"

The older woman, bless her, suddenly feeling the need to defend herself, clears her throat. "I'm the mother of the bride. I need to dress accordingly..." Little does she realize that she is playing right into her adversary's hands.

The attendant deadpans. "So mothers aren't supposed to look sexy?"

"It's just not me," the woman says, eyeing the dress on the rack.

"Then maybe you've come to the wrong department. The elderly section is upstairs..."

The woman's mouth gapes. She wasn't expecting her to say that. It's clear by the way she cocks her head. She's wondering if she heard the girl right. Surely not. She's too nice, the old woman. Maybe it's her age, but there's a certain brand of purity about her. She believes everyone is like her— kind, and unassuming, determined to do the right thing. I find it surprising that age and experience haven't knocked that right out of her, but there you have it.

"I tell you what," the attendant says, ushering the woman toward the fitting room. "How about for grins you try this one on again," she orders, "and then we can decide."

The woman looks at the dress. "This isn't even my size."

"Look—I do this all day—every day. So trust me when I say: I know your size."

The woman shakes her head but walks toward the dressing room anyway. It's amazing how often you can get a person to do what they don't want to do, simply by insisting on it. It's sad that there are so many weak people in this world, but I guess on some level, everyone seeks approval. It isn't the fact that she's weak, or the way her shoulders slope, or the way her feet slowly shuffle that gets me. It's the touch of hope in her eyes.

When the attendant turns back to me, I catch sight of her name tag. Iris, it reads, because of course it does. She's a fucking flower, this one, too good to be something plain, like a Sarah or a Jane. Her parents wanted everyone to know how special she was and finally, it's all starting to make sense. She narrows her gaze and settles in on me. "Can I help you?" she asks, and she strikes me as the kind of woman who is so insecure, so unsure of themselves, that they thrive on people telling them how great they are. The kind who eats that shit up like candy. I smile at her as though her question is the best thing I've heard all day. As though she hasn't been ignoring me, as though she isn't that which she is. She smiles back, and I let her think she's got me. Whatever I am, it's clear to her upon closer inspection that I am not what she is expecting. She's definitely one of those girls. And by *those girls,* I mean the kind that you follow on social media who post a selfie a minute and tag it with 'outfit of the day' as though everyone else in the free world doesn't put on an outfit every fucking day all the same. Not that I like social media. I don't. It's a cesspool of narcissists, and people trying to sell you things you don't need. But I follow you. Secretly, obviously. I need to know what you're up to. Anyway, you're pretty legit. Not like this one here. What are they calling them now? Snowflakes. Ah yes, that's it. This one, she's a snowflake. Not the pretty kind, that makes you want to look at it, either. No—she'd be the old kind of snow. The kind that's been around awhile. Dirty and tarnished. Full of herself— full of insecurity and self-loathing, disguised as 'oh, hey look at me.' *See me.*

I see her, all right. And what I see is that she's a dime a dozen. If not now, give her a few years...she's the kind of woman whose one true love will forever be her three cats.

"I guess you don't work on commission then," I say.

She cocks her head, as though she hasn't heard me correctly.

"I need a dress," I tell her, even though I've already made my choice.

She throws her hands up, waving them dramatically and then rolls her eyes. "You and everyone else, Mister."

"Water."

"Excuse me?"

"My name. It's Mr. Water."

"Sure it is," she sighs, although this time she eyes me up and down. "What kind of dress do you need?"

"Oh," I say glancing around, feigning confusion. "It's not for me. It's for my wife."

"So—"

"So…"

She rolls her eyes again and you know how much I love eye rollers. "So—what kind of dress does *your wife* need?"

"Hmmm," I say, drawing it out. She wasted my time and now I plan to return the favor. What can I say? I'm in a giving mood. "You mean there are different kinds?" I ask, just to fuck with her. If she can dish it, she's going to learn to take it.

She shakes her head as though she's just encountered the densest person on the planet. As though I'm the one working in a department store, hating every minute of my existence. "Evening, cocktail, casual…"

I shrug. "Evening, I guess. It's for a black-tie thing…"

"What size is she?"

"Four, I think."

She looks at me with disdain as though I'm the worst man alive for guessing at your size. Clearly, I should know these things.

"You think?"

"It's a dress. Does it need to be exact?"

"Are you serious?"

I jut out my bottom lip and wait her out.

She shifts her stance. "What's her body type?"

"Perfect."

I get the eye roll again. That makes three, if you're counting, and I am. "Lucky her."

I grin. "Lucky me."

"Well, it would help if you explain what you think qualifies as perfect, Mr. Water?"

"My wife," I say. Not just because you are, but also because there's nothing that pisses a lonely, miserable woman off more than seeing another woman who is adored.

She shoots me a look, and it's one that could kill. It confirms the sentiment and that much makes me happy. I watch her as she thinks for a second and then she walks out on the floor, where the dresses are. She doesn't beckon me to follow, she just assumes I will, and so I call her bluff.

She brings me three dresses. I hate them all. I eye the racks and point to the one I came for.

~

OF COURSE, YOU LOVE THE DRESS.

Of course, it fits just right, even if you swear it's a little tight. I tell you what I went through to get it, and you almost laugh. You swear I'm lying. But that's nothing new. You tell me it's impossible I went to a department store. But you're wrong.

Little do you know how much 'impossible' turns me on.

I recant the story of the worker and the sadness in the older woman's eyes when she gave her those slutty dresses.

"I wonder if she found a dress," you say, and it's an odd thing to ask. Also, your voice trails off. You haven't been yourself in the past few weeks, and I don't know what to do about it. Hopefully, tonight will cheer you up a bit.

"Not there," I tell you, and you look at me, and I mean *really* look at me.

You ask me to stop by the mall. You say you need a handbag.

I glance at you sideways, and I realize what a good choice I made. "A handbag? You mean a purse?"

"Yes," you confirm. "I don't have the right one," you add, and I didn't even know there was such a thing as 'the right one' but then I learn something new every day.

You go on to explain that your clutch doesn't match the dress, and you assure me that these things are important and even though I don't agree with you, I go anyway, because it turns me on when you try to convince me of bullshit with such passion in your eyes.

Also, I believe you, because so far as I know, you're not all that into handbags. Plus, I'm distracted by the thought of our night away together, about all the ways I intend to show you that dresses and handbags were never the point—that the best things in life are those that are stripped bare.

The mall is closing, and you take forever in there. I check the time. I've tried your cell three times. Each time it went straight to voicemail, and I don't know why you can't just act like a responsible adult and charge your phone.

The parking lot has emptied out, and I'm just about to go in after you. I'm so relieved I don't have to, that I don't think twice when you come strolling toward the car with that familiar glimmer in your eye.

You open the door, give me the once over and dust your hands together.

"No, Kate," I say, keeping my tone low and calm. I can't ruin our night with assumptions, no matter how good I am at getting them right. "Tell me you didn't."

You raise your brow. "I did," you reply with a smile. It's the first time I've seen a real one in weeks.

"Kate," I say again, and this time I swallow hard.

"What?" you ask, as though it's nothing. "She won't be making any more old ladies feel bad about themselves, that's for sure."

"Damn it— you know this place is crawling with cameras."

"Don't worry," you tell me, your voice as soothing as ever. "I promise, I was more careful than I've ever been."

I put the car in gear, and I get us the hell out of there. I hope for both our sake you're right.

~

IT'S DARK OUT, AND THE WIND IS BITING. I CAN'T HELP BUT BE irritated with you. You're bored, and we're later than I wanted to be, and if I hadn't brought you I wouldn't be out here not only freezing my ass off, but having to listen to you complain. I study your legs. You're right about one thing— it's too cold out here for that dress.

"How much longer?" you ask, even though I've told you a million times you don't have to wait with me. I told you to go back to the hotel, but you refuse. So, I wait. You complain. Lather. Rinse. Repeat. My mark was supposed to have left the party a half-hour ago, but then we were late, and it's possible he could have left early, and I could have missed him. In any case, his departure seems to be taking forever, considering I was assured an exact time, but it appears that like you, my source was unreliable.

You search your phone, which I've come to learn wasn't dead, just irresponsibly turned off. You're looking for news of a freshly murdered girl. "I figured out where the cameras were," you murmur. "They don't even keep them on."

Somehow I find that doubtful, but I don't say so, mostly because my mark has just come around the corner, and at least one of us has to stay focused. He isn't alone, as I was told he would be. Which as it turns out isn't just bad news, it's terrible. Not only is he not alone, he's walking hand in hand with his pregnant wife down the sidewalk, and they are walking in our direction, which is the opposite of where he's supposed to be headed. I consider calling the whole thing off, which would be the thing to do, given the number of inconsistencies, when you ask if I want you to handle it.

"No," I say, motioning toward the two of them. "We can't fuck this up. We're already running behind."

"Jude," you say, and I can hear something in your voice, something that wasn't there before, something that sounds a whole lot like ambivalence. "We can't shoot him in front of her. We can't."

"This isn't one of your fairytales, Kate. This is business," I tell you, because there's a deadline on this one, and I'm just about to miss it. If I do, it won't be good. I could offer up excuses, sure, tell the truth, that I'm inundated with jobs just like this one, guys that need to be offed by a certain date. But I'm not that kind of businessman. I don't deal in excuses.

"She's pregnant," you tell me, as though I hadn't noticed.

"Yeah— and he isn't a good guy."

You turn and you start back toward the hotel. I glance back at you. You pause, change your mind, and then walk toward me again, "If you make her watch her husband die, then neither are you."

"Tell me something I don't know," I say.

You turn and you go, and this time you don't look back.

$\approx$

"WHY, KATE? WHY?"

I feel like I say those words a lot lately. Now, is just another in a vast string of them. Thanks to you, we're seated at an entirely different black-tie event than the one we're supposed to be attending. It wouldn't have happened if you'd just let me handle my job the way I wanted to. Instead, I'm being forced to sit through some medical charity function, where there are two kinds of people: those who are drunk and those who are almost dead.

"We're supposed to be enjoying ourselves," I tell you, watching you sip your water.

You glare at me. "Aren't we?"

"No," I say. "We're babysitting a man who should be done for already."

You lick your lips. "It wasn't right."

"Making me sit through this isn't right."

You tilt your head and stick one finger in the air like you've forgotten something. "I'll be back," you say. Then you lean close and whisper in my ear. "I need to hit up the ladies room."

I wait for you through two tedious speeches and then I go looking.

As I exit the ballroom, I try your cell. It goes straight to voicemail, which can only mean two things: you're ignoring me, and you're doing it because you're up to no good. Eventually, I follow the crowd and find you standing outside the bathroom. It's clear there's chaos around you. But isn't there always?

I take you by the forearm and glance from side to side. "What's going on?"

"I don't know," you say.

I squeeze a little. Just enough to get you to talk. "Kate?"

"Fine," you lean into me. You speak in a hushed tone. You remove your arm from my grip, take me by the hand, and lead me down the hall. Eventually, I stop in front of you, refuse to go any further, and I wait.

"What?" you shrug. "I saw him go into the restroom, and I just couldn't help myself. I went in after him."

"It was my job."

"Yeah, well," you tell me, biting your lip. "Keeping the kids out of trouble was your job, too, and look how that's turned out." Your eyes widen. "We have little murderers in the making."

"What has gotten into you?" I ask, even though I know exactly what it is. You're feeling inadequate as a mother, and you're taking it out on me. You have a weak spot for revenge. You always have.

You don't say this, though. In fact, you don't answer at all. You don't speak to me again, not on our way out of the hotel, not the two blocks it takes to walk to our own, not even in the elevator on the way up. You state your position when you jut out your bottom lip and settle in for the long haul. Personally, I think this is a chicken-shit way to go about fighting, but then what do I know?

You sulk for a good hour or so, but true to form, you always find a way to prove your point. When you can't take the silence any longer, you speak. "Maybe you've just gone soft, is all."

"Maybe," I say refusing to take the bait. "But we had a plan. One in which you refused to follow. Plans keep us safe, Kate. Murdering girls in mall parking lots and choking out targets in hotel bathrooms doesn't. It's pretty simple," I tell you, shaking my head. "I don't know what I'm going to do with you. You know the rules."

"Maybe you should just kill me now and save us both the absurdity of this conversation."

"We've been over this—I'm not going there with you again…"

"Whatever—" you say. "But for the record, if you're going to kill a girl, I don't know of a better place than a mall. It's practically a serial killer's wet dream. The cops will love it too. As for your mark, well, better to let his pregnant wife think he choked on a piece of bread while taking a piss than taking a gunshot to the head, no?"

I run my hand through my hair. "You didn't plan."

You scoff and throw yours in the air. "Whatever, softy."

I seethe for a bit, wander about the room, scroll through my phone. None of it helps.

You had the chance to do this the right way, and you failed. You don't take failure lightly, which is why you're not speaking to me. It's why you simply stare at the wall.

Eventually, when I've gotten the sense that enough is enough, I go to you. There are better ways to punish you than the silent treatment.

If you think I'm soft—fine. I'll show you soft.

"That was unexpected," you say afterward, as you stare at the ceiling.

I haven't caught my breath, so I don't say anything.

You prop yourself up on one arm; you're all in now. I can tell by the way you stare at me expectantly. "What now?"

"Now, I show you that you're wrong. I haven't gone soft."

You raise your brow and offer the slightest of smiles. "I thought you just did."

～

CHAPTER SIX

KATE

You were right. A night away did help and I won't lie—it felt good to kill those people. But I can't say I didn't think of her most of the time. It's tough to be away. At home I can watch her on the monitor. It helps me feel at ease about leaving her all alone in that room. But away from home, where I can't see her, well, my mind runs wild. Literally. I obsess, wondering what she's doing—if she's hungry— if she's missing me, too.

I kept imagining that I'd stayed in. Like an old film, the images kept playing in my mind. I put the kids to bed, made popcorn, she and I took in a movie, but not the chick flick kind, because we aren't shallow like that. No, it was something deep, something we'd spend hours dissecting and discussing until it turned into an all-nighter. A slumber party — the kind I'd always wanted as a kid. You said I was distracted, and when I tried to explain, you wanted to hear nothing of it. You couldn't care less. It's sort of like when Olivia was a baby, leaving her for the first time. You say this isn't healthy, all this thinking and talking about her. But that's because you're a man, and you don't have feelings. You tell me I'm wrong, that absence makes the heart grow fonder. But how you expect me to buy this misogynist bullshit, I'll never understand.

She's become like a part of me, an extension, if you will—and I couldn't wait to tell her all about all I'd done. That's what made it so great. Also, enough time has gone by, I feel like she's learned her lesson about the incident with all the water by now. I'm sure staring at those walls and eating those horrible dried meals has taught her a thing or two about fucking with my generosity. That's the good news.

The bad news is I knew we wouldn't make it home in time for me to take her coffee. This sucked because I know it's her favorite part of the day, and I hated that she'd have to miss it all because you wanted to sleep in. In the end, I probably shouldn't have obsessed so much. It turned out to be okay. You made up for it in the hotel shower; you gave me something else to obsess over. I apologized, which took a lot —I wanted you to see that I can be giving, too. I hope I don't sound ungrateful about your surprise, and the hotel, and the fact that you pretty much let me do your job for you by killing those people, because I'm not. The thing is, no matter how much I like Cheryl and our little chats, one thing is for sure, she could never fuck me the way you do. A sentiment, I might add, you made sure to hammer in.

TO MAKE UP FOR MISSING OUR MORNING COFFEE DATE, I BRING home a chocolate croissant from breakfast at the hotel. I recall her telling me a story early on about how he would bring her chocolate croissants, and I thought it would kill two birds with one stone by showing there are no hard feelings over the great flood. Even though there kind of are.

But I need to talk to her about everything, about the

killings, and about Brady, and so I'm willing to put it behind us. The croissants should have been a nice touch. I thought they'd show her how good I can be at forgiveness. That's not what happened at all.

I tell her about last night, and I wait for questions, for the excitement to come. It never does, and she doesn't ask any questions. "You're disappointed," I remark, showing her a picture on my phone I took of you while you were sleeping.

"That's weird," she says, although I don't know why. She doesn't even glance at it, which is how I know she's just being mean. "What?" I ask, rubbing the back of my neck. "It's not weird. I just love him, that's all."

"You should."

I narrow my eyes. "It was...nice being together... It was good being a part of his world," I tell her, and I roll my neck. "I've missed that."

"What about you Kate," she asks looking up at me.

"What do you mean?"

Her expression is blank. "I've heard nothing about you... I haven't seen you in three days and so far all I've heard is Jude this and Jude that."

I smile then. I get it. She's jealous. Sometimes it's hard for me to read other people's emotions, but for her, I'm willing to do better. I know what she needs. She needs a story. So, I tell her about how I saved the pregnant woman from having to watch her husband be murdered in cold blood, and how I made it look like an accident instead, and how I'm sure knowing he died eating something he loved is better than bleeding out on a dark street.

I glance at you on my phone, or rather your photo, while she chews on what I've just said. When I look up, she's gazing off into a distance that doesn't exist.

"What?" I sigh heavily.

She looks up at me, her mouth parted. "I don't see the silver lining, is all."

I see. I take a moment to process what she might be feeling. It isn't like it is with you. With you, I can feel my way through. Maybe that's what love is, the ability to decipher another person so easily. Maybe it's the hypersensitivity to their needs, the kind that comes from nowhere, and everywhere, all the same. I rub at my jaw and tilt my head. Suddenly, I see. She wants to know me better. She wants to understand what makes me tick. "Just think—" I start and I choose my words carefully. "That girl won't be offending any more old ladies," I add and then I catch myself because I know some women can be sensitive about their age and I hope she's not one of them. "I mean, you know how trying on clothes can suck. That lady deserved happiness. Not some bitter woman hell-bent on making herself feel better at someone else's expense…"

"Really," she remarks. "Isn't that what you did?"

"No," I say. I crack my knuckles. "It's completely different." I don't know what's gotten into her. She's never this unappreciative.

"I'm sorry you're angry," I tell her, and I know I need to be a little softer, after all, I can see how much she's missed me. "I thought about you the whole time, I did. And I felt bad about leaving you alone, and you not having your coffee. So I brought you this—" I offer, pointing to the croissant. "And it's like you don't even care."

"It's stale," she says nonchalantly.

I throw my hands up. "What the hell is wrong with you?"

"Nothing—it's just that you waltz in here and brag about killing people and you know… well, you want to know what's wrong?" she asks, and she pauses to glare at me. "What's wrong is that it negates all the work we've done here, Kate. I thought I was helping. But clearly, I'm not."

"You are helping."

"I don't know," she sighs. She cocks her head and looks me up and down. "Maybe I was wrong about you. Maybe that woman at your party was right. Maybe you don't have any aspirations of your own."

I squeeze my eyes shut. By this point most people would be dead. I don't like fighting with her. "What is that supposed to mean?"

I listen as she lets out a long, slow, heavy sigh. I hear the disappointment in it. She wants to give up on me. "All I hear from you is what Jude wants. I never hear you talk about what you want." She shrugs. "I can't help but wonder if you have any kind of life of your own—if you even want that for yourself."

"I have a life."

"Maybe—" she states. "But it won't be like this forever, you know. He's going to trade you up. Men like him always do. Just make sure you have something to fall back on, is all I'm saying. Because somehow I don't think killing women in mall parking lots or building your husband's résumé is going to cut it."

I want to hit her. Actually, I want to kill her. Before I do, I reach down, pick up my croissant and go. It's hard to walk away. For now, I just need to think. I need to do what you're always telling me to do. I need to show the both of you I'm capable of not making any rash decisions.

As much as I hate to admit it, you weren't wrong. I need to stay away from her for a bit. Let's hope for her sake you're right about the other thing—let's hope absence does in fact make the heart grow fonder. Otherwise, she's in real trouble.

~

TWO DAYS LATER, YOU AND I ARE IN THE GROCERY STORE

picking up dinner when we run into the new kid on the block, Vanessa. She's not actually a kid, obviously. But she's dressed like one. "We need to hurry," I mention over your shoulder. You nod, but I don't think you're listening. Not yet anyway. You're not much of a fan of Vanessa's either. But she's a natural. It was easy for her, she was accepted immediately and without question by our friends and neighbors. I didn't like it. However, I've been so busy with Cheryl, that rather than do anything about it, I've sat back and watched. It's almost impressive, the way she has so easily inserted herself. Also, Liv really seems to like her daughter, despite all the prodding I attempted in other directions. So, basically it's safe to say, my distaste for her is messy.

The moment I see her from the corner of my eye, I pull the evade and avoid method. "Come on," I tell you, tugging at your sleeve. You're staring at your phone and so you don't pay me much attention, which is clear when the next time you round an aisle you practically ram your basket right into her.

"Easy cowboy," she says, touching her throat. She breaks out into a grin, and I'd love to knock that smug look off her face. I stuff my hands in the pockets of my jeans instead. This might be the hardest thing I've ever done. But I don't think grocery stores are ideal for murder, not with their open aisles and fluorescent lighting. Needless to say, I'm still bitter about the other night. Also, there's just the simple fact that I don't like her. In my mind, I picture myself slitting her throat, stuffing her lifeless body in a cart and rolling her out to the trunk. I force a smile instead, hoping I don't have to go to the trouble, hoping she'll keep her mouth shut, and we can be on our merry way. You, on the other hand, don't have to force anything. I guess it doesn't hurt that she's wearing nothing but a too-short tennis skirt and sports bra IN THE GROCERY STORE.

"How embarrassing—" she starts rubbing her throat. "Running into you guys like this." I imagine replacing her hand with mine and squeezing until every bit of her is gone. "Look at me—" she exclaims and boy are you ever. "All sweaty and gross. I've just come from tennis…I just *knew* I should have changed," she says loudly. "But what can you do?" she asks, her voice raising, clearly doing the opposite of what she says she wants to do—drawing attention to herself —and I can think of a few things *I'd* like to do. You seem to sense my irritation; I can tell by the way you place your hand over mine. "It's hard to fit it all in," she drones on. You don't say anything, which is only because she's half-naked; usually you excel at cutting off conversations you don't want to have.

"Tell me about it," I say, looking at you.

"I just ran in to pick up a few things…I'm making something special tonight and needed a good wine to pair with it, and I was SURE I wouldn't run into anyone. But that's how these things work, isn't it?"

"Apparently so," I say, but she's looking at you.

She claps her hands together as though everything suddenly makes sense. " Anyway," she smiles, "we're celebrating—I finally made partner!"

Of course she did. I widen my eyes and close my lips, pressing them together until I feel them go numb. "Congratulations," you tell her.

"Wow," I offer, and it's about as fake as her boobs. "That's great."

She shrugs and rises up on to her tippy toes, stretching, and what the fuck is happening here? "Blood, sweat and tears…it always pays off…"

"Mostly, the blood," I say.

"Speaking of blood," she mentions, furrowing her brow. "Did you hear?" She lowers her voice and leans in closer to you as she asks the question. It's like she's a cat, trying to rub her scent on you, begging you to pet her, begging for attention. She doesn't even hide it.

"Hear what?" you ask, and you look at me. You're grinning. You know exactly what I'm thinking. I'm thinking she's going to have to die after all. Right here and now in the middle of this store. It will suck to see such a great pair of legs go to waste— must be those calf raises she does in random places like aisle six in the grocery store—but what can you do?

"How could you not hear?" she demands loudly. "Have you been living under a rock?"

"Something like that," I say, but you only shrug and stare at her tits. I want to blame you, but I can't. Her bra is neon pink, which means they're practically blinking on and off every time she breathes.

"Anyway," she tells you and the rest of the store. "The girl they found at the mall…the media is saying it might be some sort of serial killer."

"Hmmm," you say, and it's sad that you can't do better than that. You can't help yourself, you're hypnotized.

"Can you imagine? Right here in our little town…" she adds, and she shivers, which causes her oversized tits to shake. You take ample notice.

"No," I tell her. "I can't."

She shakes her head slowly. Her tits go too. "The cops don't have any leads either…which is terrible," she says, her eyes bulging. "I mean, especially given this is like the fourth one…"

I cock my head. Finally she has said something worthwhile. "The fourth one?"

"Yeah, you know—all those girls."

I jut out my bottom lip and narrow my brow. I need to know more. You stare at your phone.

"God, you really have been living under a rock," she sighs.

"Anyway— they think he's meeting them online. I mean… just because it's so random and all. Well, that… and one of them told her roommate she was meeting some guy for hookup sex."

"Hookup sex. Huh," I say, and the wheels are turning.

"Yeah, apparently that sort of thing is all the rage these days. There's like an app. Just for hooking up."

"Really?" you say, and you look up from your phone but I'm pretty sure you weren't actually listening.

"I hadn't heard…" I tell her.

"We don't watch the news," you confess, and maybe I was wrong. I guess you were listening.

"I probably shouldn't either," she mentions, her tone serious. "Now I can't sleep. Anyway, talk about career goals! That would be something—catching the guy who's doing this —for any cop, that would be amazing," she mentions, which makes no sense. "Personally, I think they need to offer reward money."

"Maybe…" I reply.

"But the girls, well, it's just so sad. I mean how bad off do things have to be to just pick up your phone and agree to meet some random stranger for sex?"

You don't respond, although I'm interested to hear what you'd say. Would you agree or would you set her straight? I'll never know, because you're staring at your phone again.

"I don't know," I offer. "To each their own, I guess."

"You're funny, Kate," she tells me, because she thinks I'm being sarcastic when really I'm just not judgmental like she is. "Any who—" she quips. "I'd better run. I promised I'd make David's favorite tonight…and God knows how that man hates waiting."

You look up and you nod.

"Say," she mentions. "You guys should join us."

I shake my head. "We can't tonight. Jude leaves town

again tomorrow morning…"

You smile. "But a rain check would be nice," you add, and if I weren't so intrigued by everything she's just said I might just kill you both.

~

THE TRUTH IS, I'VE BEEN A LITTLE BUMMED OUT. THEY FINALLY let Brady go back to school, although I know this isn't the end of it. It doesn't help that all the other mothers are whispering and looking at me funny, even though to my face they tell me they know that little shit Matthew is a bully and something needs to be done about it.

I want to ask Cheryl what to do. But I can't even do that. It's been four days since I've been to see her. She's surviving on MREs, and if I'm lucky, guilt. I've been thinking that maybe Vanessa was right at our dinner party, which is the other part of the problem. All of this sitting around is beginning to get to me. It's making me question everything. Plus, I saw the way you looked at Vanessa in the store, and it made me think Cheryl is right, too. Maybe I am replaceable. Then there was the dig Vanessa made about having career goals. Both she and Cheryl aren't too far off; I don't have a life of my own. I have no real purpose. I'm just a mom. A mom who has one real friend in the whole world—unless you count Josie, and I don't. Josie isn't a friend. She's a fan, and they're not exactly one and the same.

I don't want to be a nobody, Jude. I don't. I want to be someone who does something great with her life, something worthy, someone everyone likes— someone people look up to. Not a PTA committee leader, a glorified volunteer, someone everyone pities because she works so hard for free just to keep her hands busy, just so people can think she's proving her worth. That's pathetic. That's what I've become.

And I intend to spend every ounce of energy I have fixing this.

I'm too bummed to go up and see her. I'm not ready to concede. I mean, sure, she's right. I'm getting better. The nightmares have all but vanished and the voices have stayed away. But somehow that's not enough. I think I just need another day. Another day to plan, another day to get my thoughts together, another day to make sure she knows what it means to suffer the way I am.

I spend most of the first day you're away on business reading up on history's greats. Let's call it research. Turns out, research gets boring quick. You see, that's the thing. I don't want to be just another version of someone else. I want to be something new, someone better. And that's when it hits me: I don't learn by research; I learn by doing.

I think on it, and I decide I know what—no— who I want to be. It's risky, and you won't like it, but then no one ever proved anything by playing it safe, and of course, no one said you have to know.

It's easy peasy—the becoming, the planning—this new life I intend to lead. Almost too easy. First, I create a fake email account. I sign myself in as Kimmy T online, on one of those 'hookup sites' Vanessa mentioned. *Looking to hookup. I like it rough.* I press the keys, make the words come to life on the screen, like it's nothing, and then because I know the serial type, I add *Weird ones only need reply.* I add a photo of myself, tap a button on my screen, and just like that, it's done.

Of course, I post a picture of someone else—it's a stock photo, but to my credit, I do choose one that at least looks like me.

Three hours later, I'm pleasantly surprised. Although I guess I really shouldn't be. There are four hundred and eighty-six responses waiting in my inbox. It's insane, when you think about it. Results like that. I could be busy for a while if I wanted. After all, there's nothing worse than a man who gets off on hurting women. Not just hurting them, but killing them, like it's nothing.

I read through the responses, my excitement growing more and more with each one. It's a tough call, but in the end, my time is limited, with you away and having to get the kids looked after, so I have to choose carefully. 'Mr. Right,' seems like as good a choice as any. His profile tells me everything I need to know: He's a loner, a self-proclaimed mama's boy, married to his work, not looking for anything serious. He fits the bill of a killer, to a T. Calling himself 'Mr. Right,' tells me he's a classic narcissist, albeit an honest one, and he's smart. He knows that his words, no matter how true they might be, will make the majority of women think he is a challenge. He checks all the boxes. He knows his type, which is pretty much every woman with low enough self-esteem that they're willing to buy his brand of bullshit. He's a joke. A character right out of a bad romance novel. Also, a joke that is too hard not to turn down. With a response that read: 'Want it rough? I'm your man.' in the subject line, no less, he did seem like 'Mr. Right.'

At his suggestion, we meet in a parking garage downtown. Interestingly, he's younger than I imagined. I envisioned some creep rolling up, inviting me into his car, into his twisted mind, but what I get instead is some middle-aged man so nondescript that I probably wouldn't glance twice if I saw him on the street. "Mr. Right?" I ask, climbing into the passenger seat.

"That's me," he replies.

My eyes narrow. I haven't focused this hard on reading anyone or anything in four long days. "What a pleasure."

He looks me up and down. "It will be for me," he says and then he sort of does this thing with his throat. It isn't a laugh and it isn't a moan, it's awkward is what it is.

"I just hope you're as tough as you let on in your email…" he tells me, putting his sports car in gear. He revs the engine, and it strikes me as odd that he wants to be noticed at a time like this, but sometimes the reason people do what they do is anybody's guess. He looks over at me then, and okay, I have to admit there is a little bit of a creep factor there when I think about it. He takes the corners like they're nothing, he makes it obvious he wants to show me what this car can do, and I couldn't be more turned off if I tried. "Like I said," he adds. "I can be pretty rough—I don't want no softy."

"I can assure you— I'm not soft," I say before I instruct him to drive out to the barn. "I know a place," I tell him. "I have supplies there." He already knows this though. I'm just reiterating what I've said in our prior correspondence.

"How can I be sure you're not 5-0?" he asks.

I laugh. "I'm a little closer to 4-0 these days," I say and he furrows his brow. My age bothers him. Men like him always want younger, with less experience.

"Spunk, huh…" he comments several minutes later. I know because I'm staring at the clock. "It's good," he nods, like he's realized something. "That makes it more fun."

"Always," I say.

"Anyway," he swallows. "Just to be clear—we're not exchanging money for this— so nothing illegal is taking place," he says karate chopping the air with his hand. "I want to make sure there are no misconceptions here."

"We're two consenting adults," I say.

"Exactly," he replies, and he seems pleased with my lingo. Soon I'll find out why.

"Also, this isn't a relationship. I'm not looking for that. I'm quite happy with my wife."

"I figured as much," I reply although I hadn't considered that he might have a wife. I wish he hadn't brought that part up, because it makes me sad for her having to live with this.

He doesn't say anything else. Not for a while. He's already questioned me on my likes and dislikes, and mostly about how far he can go. *All the way, I promised him. All the way.* When we're close, he whips out a piece of paper. It startles me, the sudden movement, and I reach for the gun I have in the holster on my thigh. Thankfully, I see it's paper he's shoving in my direction, and I relax my arm. He pushes the stack my way. "It's a consent form," he says. After that, he hands over a non-disclosure agreement.

"Turn right," I say glancing at the paperwork. I wonder where he keeps the rest of them. It seems kind of dangerous to retain all of that evidence, if you ask me. Truthfully, it's a blow. He takes the corner hard.

"I'm an attorney," he tells me glancing over. I keep my eye on the paperwork.

"Of course, you are," I say grabbing the pen from his hand. I sign on the dotted line. It's almost too bad. This isn't the guy. The guy I'm looking for wouldn't ask me to sign paperwork if he were just going to kill me.

Oh, well. I'm feeling a bit of rage at choosing wrong and thinking of telling Cheryl about this excites me. He may not be 'Mr. Right' in the way that matters, I may not be taking a killer off the streets tonight, but he seems like as good a distraction as any.

"You don't have any questions for me? No small talk?" he asks looking me up and down once more.

"Nope," I reply and I shift in my seat, staring straight ahead. "Keep your eyes on the road."

"Right," he says. "We wouldn't want some silly little accident spoiling our fun."

"No," I agree. "We wouldn't."

~

CHAPTER SEVEN

JUDE

I'm halfway across the country in some no name town in Vermont and you're God knows where. I know because I've tried your cell five times. The sixth time I call Josie instead. She tells me she has the kids and so far as she knows you're at home 'working.'

"Working on what?"

"Oh, so you haven't heard?" she asks and I brace myself. "Kate is writing a novel."

I almost laugh. "Is that so?"

"Yes," she says and it's amazing. She believes your lies. "I'm hoping she'll let me read it… but she says I have to wait till the second draft. It's so hard waiting, isn't it?"

It sure as shit is, I want to say. But I don't.

A novel. That's cute, you know. Very, very cute.

Now, where in the fuck are you, really?

~

I TRY YOUR CELL AGAIN. I HAVE TIME ON MY HANDS, LOTS OF time to kill, given that the guy I've been hired to kill is going to be late. His flight was delayed and sitting around some cozy bed and breakfast wondering what you're up to, isn't doing it for me. I decide to go for a walk but I quickly realize I underestimated this kind of cold. I go left when my gut tells me to go right, and I zip my coat up tighter. It doesn't make much difference though. The wind cuts to the bone, it's visceral. I don't know where I'm headed, all I know is I couldn't stay in that room another minute. The old woman at the front desk told me there's a tavern in town, but I know I can't go there, as it is I've already shown my face around more than I should've. Murder doesn't happen in towns like these, and they don't take too kindly to strangers. They're friendly only in the way that they want to know what you've come for and how soon you're leaving. Telling them you're a real estate developer makes them like you less. I've made that mistake a time or two, so now I just say that I'm just passing through on my way to the city and since I'm from the south, I don't like to drive in snow, in the dark. They like that story, it's the kind of lie that makes sense. It also raises the stakes. People in little towns talk, so if you're going to take one of their own out, you'd better make damn sure you get away with it. Thankfully there's a plan in place for that.

I walk on, past the summer homes, all closed up for winter, and the further on I go, the clearer it becomes how desolate the town is. I pass an old farmhouse. It's the kind of home you'd like, in warmer weather. I stop and stare at it, and then I realize why. It looks a lot like the house I grew up in. From the short picket fence to the green swing-set that looks as though it hasn't been used in years, it feels very familiar. Minus all the snow. I picture the house as it might look in the summer, with dew-drenched grass, and lightning bugs floating across the lawn, and all of a sudden, I really need to hear your voice.

◠

"HE'S NOT COMING BACK THIS TIME, I KNOW IT," MY MOTHER tells me. She's sitting in my dad's recliner, no one ever does, and she's convinced. I know because she's used the word eight times in the last hour alone. "I'm convinced—this is it," she repeats again. She pulls her knees up to her chest and rocks back and forth. Back and forth.

"He's coming back," I promise, even though I'm not at all sure. He isn't answering my calls either. He left a number, but all I get is the operator lady telling me I've misdialed.

"You don't know him like I do," she tells me, and she's right. Also, I'm only seven. It's hard to know anyone at that age. "I think we should have a moment of silence, son."

"What's a moment of silence?"

She stares at the wall, and maybe through it, too. "It's our way of saying goodbye…"

"I don't want to do that."

"It's time you accepted it," she says going to the kitchen. I know what she's after, her favorite bottle. "It's time we both accepted it."

I watch as she pours herself a glass and then another and another. Eventually, she pours one that she doesn't immediately down. She hands it to me. "We should have a toast," she says. "To your father."

"This isn't toast."

She throws her head back and laughs. "A—toast. It's wishing someone well."

That made sense. "Okay."

She pulls another glass from the cupboard. "To the leaving kind," she says, and she clinks her glass with mine.

"You were supposed to drink."

"I don't like that stuff. It's gross. And it makes you sad."

"I'm not sad."

"Yes," I tell her. "You are."

"That's it!" she says. She tosses the glass in the sink so hard it breaks. "Out!" She presses her palm to my back and ushers me out of the kitchen, to the front door.

"You're just like him. *Just like him.* You want to go —fine—go."

"I don't want to go…"

I watch as she opens the front door and unlocks the screen door. She holds it open and points her finger. "Get out."

"But—"

My mother shakes her head. "There are no buts. Go."

I do as she says. She doesn't let me back in, not even when it gets dark. I play on my swing set and sleep in the tree house my dad made back when he was actually around.

~

I ASKED YOU TO COME, WHICH WAS PRETTY MUCH THE SAME thing as asking for trouble. When you said no, I figured it was probably just as well. Still, you know how much I dislike it when you turn me down. Being here in this cold, picturesque town alone gives me motivation to shore things up back home. I start back toward the B&B, and I make a plan. A little spite and a little revenge should do the trick. I'm weary and ready to get this job over and done with so I can hop on a plane and wing it all the way back to you.

I know it isn't ideal, the way things have been going. I get it. Your hands are full. How could you be happy, between practically living at the school and dealing with that woman? I realize I haven't been much help. I'm up to my eyeballs in work. So I'm not surprised you aren't taking my calls. You're angry. But guess what? You don't get to toy with me this way. You think my leaving is easy. You're wrong. It's hard to stay away when one thinks their wife is up to no good—and you're always up to something.

I'm up to something, too. It's called earning a living. I'm not here to take leisurely strolls around scenic old neighborhoods. I'm here to kill another 'big pharma guy,' an associate of the man you choked out in a hotel bathroom. It wasn't my job to begin with, it was my former (almost) associates, the man you practically forced me to take out. It sort of becomes a given when you abduct a hitman's wife. It'd be nice if I weren't still bitter about the whole thing, but what can I say? I'd be home with my family, where I belong, if you were a less impulsive woman. To the contrary, I'm standing in the middle of a man's house with my gun aimed directly at 'Big Pharma's' left temple when my cell rings. I could just pull the trigger, and I should, but the thing is, I've been waiting for your call.

"Jude," you say in a hushed tone. You don't wait for me to say hello.

I press the gun to the man's temple, silently warning him not to make a move. He won't. He's not the type.

"Where in the fuck are you? I've called eight times."

"I'm afraid there's been a situation."

"A situation? What kind of situation?"

"Please," he begs. "I'll give you whatev—"

I hit him upside the head with my gun. I don't like violence for the sake of violence. But it shuts him up, so there is that. "On your knees," I order.

"What?" you say. Your voice is muffled.

"Nothing."

You inhale. "If one needed to dispose of a car…" you start. "How might one go about that?"

My guy leans forward. He's testing me. I grab his hair, yank him back. Then I steady the barrel on his temple once again. This time I make sure to apply a little more pressure.

"Whose car?" I take a deep breath in, hold it, and let it out. *Why must you always have this effect on me?* "Dear God Kate—"

"Just tell me what to do. I'm not thinking clearly…"

'Pharma' tries to stand. I was wrong about him and about leaving town. I was wrong in thinking I could trust the both of you not to try something stupid. You know how I hate being wrong. He manages to take off running, but he stumbles on his expensive rug. I'd be willing to bet he has a bit of buyer's remorse right about now. "This isn't a good time, actually…" I say, shoving the phone in my jacket. I start after him. He doesn't get far. It helps my cause that he's more than a tad out of shape. I guess people don't consider the odds of outrunning an assassin when they shove that third slice of pizza down their throat. It's too bad, really.

"Are you still there?" I ask, fishing the phone out of my pocket and placing it to my ear. I got him. He's out of breath, and I'm out of patience.

"I'm here," you say. You sound tired.

I click the safety but mostly I watch my guy. "So this car…"

"Yeah—what do I do with it?"

"Where are you?"

"At the barn."

"The barn?" I repeat. This isn't what I wanted to hear. I pull him by his collar to the far edge of the rug. I consider the splatter and tug just a little more until he's right where I want him to be. I position my gun and pull the trigger.

"What was that?"

"Business."

"You're doing a job? Right now?

"*Was* doing a job," I correct.

"What the fuck are you talking to me for, then?"

"You called," I scoff. "What'd you think I was doing? Baking a cake?"

"I don't know. Maybe running…"

"Well, that, too," I admit. "The barn… Jesus, Kate. It's eleven o'clock at night…"

"Yep."

"So, it's like that huh?"

"It's like that."

I check the poor bastard's pulse, and I grab the body bag. I'm thankful the clean up has been left to someone else. It's one of the only reasons I took this job. "Is it safe to drive it to the yard?"

"You see, that's the thing… I don't know."

"What do you mean, you don't know?"

"I mean, I don't know."

"You don't sound like yourself."

"I think I have a concussion…"

My breath catches. I should've known better than to leave town. "A concussion."

"I took a hit. No big deal."

Of course it's a big deal. With you, everything is a big deal. "Stay there. I'm calling Rudy."

"I was afraid you'd say that."

"Is there someone else I should call? A taxi?"

You don't answer, and the line goes dead.

THE FOLLOWING EVENING WHEN I ARRIVE HOME YOU'RE LYING on the couch with a blanket over your head. You aren't speaking to me, you won't take my calls, but I'm pretty aware of what I'm walking into. The kids are still with Josie, which I'm not happy about. I know I need to get over there, but I also know this has to happen first.

I sit down next to you, lift your hand, and take it in mine. I'm too tired to fight. Almost. But I'm angry, and I'm willing, because you've fucked up and you've made a fool out of me in the process. You pull away, just as I expected you would. I reach over again, this time for the other hand. Your hands are warm, and I wonder how long you've been here like this. Rudy said he thinks most of the day. I pull your arm closer and study the dirt under your fingernails. It isn't like you to leave any clues. But maybe that's because you always have me cleaning up behind you.

"You know," you say, and you pause to let out one of your signature long sighs. "I did this before you were around. I'm not an imbecile."

No, you're a mind reader, is what you are.

"Things are different now. We have children. Children who need their mother. Children who have been at the neighbors for the past two days—children who spend about twenty percent of their time at someone else's house."

"She likes having them there."

"That's not the point."

"She can't have more kids, Jude. You know that. Why not let her be happy? Why do you insist on making everyone unhappy?"

That was a low blow, and if you're going to hit hard, you're going to look me in the eye when you do it. I pull the blanket away from your face. *Damn.* I inhale audibly. Rudy hasn't told me it's this bad. It hurts to look at you. Your left eye is practically swollen shut. There's dried blood at the corner of your nose and your lip is split. All things that will heal in time, I know this. But it doesn't make me feel any better now. I reach in to touch your eye. You flinch. "How did this happen? Wait—first— just tell me the motherfucker who did it is dead."

You tilt your head. "You know he is. I'm sure your father told me how he had to save my ass," you say, and you're right. I did know. Still, there's something about hearing you say it that I seem to need right now. Considering your condition, I'd say I deserve a little peace of mind. You've always been good at getting yourself into trouble, but not like this.

"How did this happen?"

"It doesn't matter," you reply and you look away. "The outcome is the same regardless, isn't it?"

"It does matter."

"Fine," you say looking me in the eye. "He hit me in the head— it threw me off— I recovered—he's dead—all is well."

"All is hardly well. Look at your face, goddammit. You have a concussion, and I had to call my father to rescue you."

"*Nice.* I knew it wouldn't take long for you to throw that in my face."

"I'm sorry, Kate," I tell you throwing up my hands. "But you know how he worries."

"Worries for who? Not for me."

"He showed up, didn't he?"

You don't respond.

I pinch the bridge of my nose. "I need to know this isn't going to happen again."

"I don't know what to tell you," you say, and you know that phrase is like nails on a chalkboard to me which I'm pretty certain is why you say it.

"What you are going to tell me is that you won't be messing around with men anymore. You won't be taking them out to the barn, and you sure as hell won't be doing it while I'm out of town."

"Messing around with men…" you scoff. "Well, that's one way to put it."

"Promise me, Kate."

"I won't mess around with men while you're out of town."

I study your face, and I shake my head. You are relentless. The worst part is, other than locking you in that panic room with your little pet, I haven't the slightest idea what I'm going to do about it.

∼

"No more men, son," my father tells me. I'm around eleven, he picked me up from school, which he never does, which is how I know whatever he's about to tell me is important. I know because I remember staring at the words to *Bridge to Terabithia,* and we read that book in the fifth grade. I turn the words over in my mind, anything to avoid meeting his gaze. "If you see any other man around this house, no matter what your mother tells you, I want you to pull out my gun. Don't shoot the bastard— but don't let him think you won't, either."

"Yes, sir," I tell him without looking up.

He exhales slowly. "I know this is a lot to ask of you."

I raise my eyes to his then, because I know it's the only way for this conversation to end quickly.

"I talked to Bob last week. We both agree…it's time to start really training you up."

"What is that supposed to mean?" I ask, although I'm sure I have a pretty good idea. My father and I flew to Bob's place once, in Sri Lanka, and all I remember about that trip is how hot and muggy it was and how much I looked forward to getting back home.

"It means that you're ready. That—and it would do you some good to get away from here for a summer. See the world a bit."

I close my book. "I like it here."

"Bob is retired, son. He can watch out for you."

"I can watch out for myself."

I watch his jaw set and I know he isn't going to budge. "Yes, I know," he says. "That's what I'm afraid of."

~

CHAPTER EIGHT

KATE

"You're coming with me," you say, throwing my things in a bag. It's early afternoon, and the thought of going through one more day like this threatens to do me in. I don't want to fight anymore—if fighting is what you call not speaking to one another—I don't want to live this way. And if irritation has its limit, when I see you standing there without a shirt on, packing my stuff, I know I've reached mine. It's hard to stay mad at a person when they look like you.

"Where are we going?"

"San Francisco."

I let my shoulders drop. "I hate California. You know that."

"It isn't a question, Kate," you say, looking at me with equal parts confusion and amusement. "Clearly, I can't leave you alone. Not unless I want to end up a widower raising two kids on my own."

"So, you do love me after all," I lament, and I can't help breaking out into a grin. The sun has come out again, and you want my help. It's sweet that you think you know what I need to make me feel better, to make me whole again, and that thing is a kill.

You break eye contact. "Why else would I insist you come with me?"

I lean in and I kiss you. It's a test. You pass.

"I don't understand you at all..." you offer, watching my eyes. I raise my brow. You shake your head, take me by the shoulders, and turn me around. I watch your reflection in the mirror and then your hands as they trail lower, caressing me, slipping down the front of my yoga pants. "Let's not fight anymore, okay?"

I nod and then you push me forward, until I'm pressed up against the dresser. When you lower your hand against my back and push down, forcing me to bend over, I go willingly. You don't take your eyes off me, and when I try to close mine because staring back at you in that mirror is too much, you demand that I look at you. You make me feel things I don't want to feel. Take forgiveness, for example. But mostly, you make up for all the distance there's been between us these past few days. You aren't particularly sweet or soft in your method; you don't take it easy. But I'm not one to complain. You always seem to know exactly what I want, and it should make me happy, but it doesn't, because this time you're quick, which isn't like you. It gives your feelings away. You're still angry with me. Afterward you try not to let it show when you turn me around, take my face in your hands, and look me directly in the eye. "What is happening to me?" you ask. I don't say anything, but it's a good question. "Am I meant to be mad Kate, and if so, why do you have to make it so hard?"

I smile, because I like it when you get all poetic on me. That sated look in your eye doesn't hurt any either. I shrug, because I don't know what else to say. There's a lot I could mention. I ruminate on it instead.

Eventually, we sink down to the floor, where you slip your fingers in mine, and I stare at a loose thread in the rug. I think about what we've just done, how we're so broken, and yet we fit just right. You stand and you reach your hand down, offering it to me. I take it, and you pull me up. You wrap your hand around the back of my neck. "Come lay down with me," you say and then you direct me where you want me to go. You could've asked me to go to hell, to the moon, anywhere, and I think I might say yes. It's a curious thing, I think, making my way over to the bed, the way a person's hand can fit so perfectly around the back of your neck. The way it can grip you— let you know exactly who you are and where you are meant to fit in the world.

Later, as we're lying together, I look down at your hand on mine. I pick it up and bring it toward my face, and I study your palm. There's nothing quite like the way it feels when it's pressed against my windpipe—it feels right— like everything in the universe is just as it's meant to be. Would I suffocate to feel this for eternity? I think I might. This feeling— you—it's lovely— and it's hell. I look up, and I can't help but wonder how we're back here again in this all too familiar predicament—love-drunk, swallowed whole, ready to die for such a thing as love. Not only ready—but eager to do it.

I don't tell you any of this, though. I don't tell you about my goals of catching the man who is killing those girls. I don't tell you about my plans for the woman in the room upstairs. In fact, I hardly think about any of that stuff at all. I soak this feeling up instead. We both know there'll be plenty of time for all the other stuff later.

∾

I CLOSE MY EYES, AND JUST LIKE THAT, I'M SIX YEARS OLD

again and back in that room. It's like time travel, and it's very, very real.

I'm never going to get out of here, I say to myself, brushing matted hair out of my eyes. I'm cold and hungry and too tired to sleep. I tell myself that, too. It helps to say these things out loud. It's nice to hear a voice, even if it happens to be my own. I shut my eyes, squeezing them hard. I'm at the point of giving up. It doesn't help, it just reminds me of what landed me in here in the first place. I have to remember. I force myself. It helps that it gives me something to think about. Also, I don't want to make the same mistake again. Never make the same mistake twice, Daddy always says.

"Can we have spaghetti for dinner?" I'd asked my dad on his way out that morning.

"We'll see," he said, buttoning his coat.

"Make sure to listen for your mother. And don't forget—I'm warning you—call me if she comes out, all right?"

"When do I get to go to school Daddy?" I ask, because I'm thinking about him leaving, about having to spend another day in this house alone. Shelly gets to go to school, and it sounds like fun. "I want to be like Shelly."

"You do not want to be like Shelly," he says disapprovingly. "Now, run along." Shelly is my cousin, but we don't see her much anymore. Not since she put ideas about school in my head. Daddy says school is for imbeciles, even though I don't know what that means. He says it's a place where future factory workers go. People like Shelly and that stupid brother of his. We aren't like them, he reminds me, like he always does if I ask.

"Don't forget…spaghetti…" I tell him, imagining the feel of the noodles on my tongue. I've only had it just the once, so it's special, and Daddy knows this. It's why he smiles. Or maybe it's the thought of my mother, the way she looked as she made it. That was 367 days ago now—back when I was still five. I mark the days on the calendar. It gives me something to do, something other than watch TV. I know I'm not supposed to, so sometimes I don't, I just look at the calendar on the fridge instead and I work out the days in my head. 298 days until Christmas. Sometimes for the fun of it, I look at 'spaghetti day' on the calendar. She was so patient, so loving that day; I think it should be a holiday, too. It was like most of them. Not all good and not all bad.

"It's the new doctor," my father said bitterly. He wanted none of our special recipe. "He's got you cooking, pretending, trying to be normal. That is a quack and what does that make you? Letting him put all these ideas in your head…"

My mother hadn't said anything. She continued sucking noodles into her mouth. It was rare to see her eat, so it was kind of nice.

I like the idea of spaghetti. Maybe that doctor is the worst thing that could've happened, like he said. Eventually, he took the plate from her, tossed it in the sink, and turned on the water. "Enough," he said, but he let me have mine.

After that day I asked for it on a regular basis. My mother never cooked again. Then yesterday, my father brought home a grocery bag, turned it over and let the contents fall onto the kitchen counter. "If you want spaghetti so bad," he said. "Make it yourself."

I studied the items, and I tried to remember. I could do it, I told myself. It would sure beat eating cereal again. Plus, maybe it would cheer mom up, maybe she'd come out of that room. It'd been sixteen days now.

"I don't know what to do with the two of you," he tells me. "She thinks that clown is helping her—well—I'll be damned if any wife of mine is talking to another man about her "problems." You wanna know what the problem is…the problem is that she sits on her fat ass all day and does NOTHING. THAT'S HER FUCKING PROBLEM."

"She won't come out anymore, Daddy."

"You don't need her, Lydia," he says.

"I like it when she makes spaghetti. I'm tired of cereal…"

He considers what I've just said, and then he smiles. It isn't a nice smile. He doesn't have too many of those kind these days. "That's why I brought all this home, you ungrateful little rat."

I don't want to be an ungrateful rat; I don't want to make Daddy mad. Not the way she does. I don't want to go in that room. I make a promise to myself. I'm going to make spaghetti, and everyone is going to be happy again.

Turns out now, no one is happy, least of all me. It began when I spilled the pot of boiling water on myself, sloshing it across my legs, and it ended when I landed here. I screamed, and I couldn't stop. He didn't take me to the doctor. "What are they going to do that I can't do?" he asked.

I didn't know. My dad says they just like to take people's money.

Mom finally snuck in today. Sometimes she does that. But not always. She looked wild-eyed and crazy. "Take these," she said placing two pills in my hand. "It'll help the pain."

I stare at them. Then I roll them between my fingers. "I don't know how to swallow medicine…"

"Learn," she says handing me a glass of water.

"Can you take me to the doctor? Like that time when I had the fever?"

She bites at her bottom lip. It bleeds. "Your father would kill me…"

"It hurts mommy," I say pointing to my scalded, blistered skin.

"It will heal, Lydia. Everything heals."

This makes me angry. She isn't supposed to be in here,

and she shouldn't have come, no matter how glad I am to see her. It's only going to make things worse. "Why do you have to do what he says anyway?"

She considers my question for a moment and then she lowers her gaze. "Sometimes the only way to know one's enemy is to get really close," she says and she sucks in her bottom lip. She mumbles something about fire I can't make out. "You have to get close enough to the fire to get burned. Close enough to let it kill you, my child." I don't understand what she means, my legs hurt too bad to try, and in any case, she rarely makes a lot of sense anyway. My dad says it's the pills, which is another reason I don't want to take what she's handed me. She studies the pills in my hand. "It's a nice thing to feel in control of one's fate. I think it's one of the things human beings most seek. Freedom. The power to choose how things turn out. Love is the wild card in it all, the twist of fate that throws a wrench in even the best laid plans...."

I don't say anything. I stare at the pills and I wonder if they might help my legs. I wonder if I can learn to swallow them. I wonder if I can trust him.

"I love him, Lydia," she says, and I turn away. I know what comes next. She's going to tell me he can't know she was here. She needs to go.

"I made you this," she says, placing a bowl at my feet. I ate it. But I never did like spaghetti much after that.

~

"KATE," YOU SAY SHAKING ME AWAKE. I LOOK UP AT YOU. WE'RE in the bed half-clothed, and it takes me a second to recall how I ended up here this way.

"You were talking in your sleep. Something about making spaghetti," you say, and you sort of laugh. "You hate spaghetti."

I rub at my eyes, remembering your hand pressed against my back. "I know."

You search my face. "Everything okay?"

"Fine," I say.

"Oh," you answer, brushing my hair out of my eyes. "I know you're not coming with me to California."

I purse my lips and look into your eyes. "I'm sorry," I tell you. "There's just so much going on here…"

"I know. But we have to do something about her eventually, Kate. She can't stay in that room forever."

"Okay," I huff, and I surprise myself by how annoyed I am that you bring this up now. Now, as in after my nightmare; now, as in after we've just made up.

You pat my thigh. "Let's not worry about it now. We'll take care of it when I'm back."

"Yeah," I reply, but it's half-hearted at best.

◇

I CHECK YOUR CALENDAR. YOU DON'T HAVE ANY TRIPS COMING up after this one. Not for a while—which means I have to make the best of the time you're gone. Time is running out.

"Kate," she says after we've finished our coffee. "I was wondering if you've given anymore thought to what I've asked?"

I sigh, because we've been over this, and because I know what she wants from me.

"Yes," I tell her. "I've just been swamped…"

"I get it. But you know—a deal *is* a deal. And that husband of yours…well, he seems pretty unpredictable, and I for one would like to die knowing that you held up your end of the bargain."

"All right," I tell her, and my voice comes out harsh. "I said I'd go see him. And I will."

She looks relieved. She looks like she's going to let it go. Sometimes she surprises me. I hope this is one of those times.

By him, she is referring to her lover, and she knows I hate talking about this, so I don't know why she insists on bringing it up every time I come to see her.

"Just promise me that whatever happens, you'll get the book back to him."

"I'll make sure he gets the book," I promise, when the truth is, I don't really give a shit about the book. It was never about him or the book. But she made me agree that if she were going to help me, then a trade was in order, and that's what she's referring to now. It's what she always refers to before our session. *Him.*

"I will take care of it," I repeat. "Things have just been so busy around here lately."

She presses her lips to one another. "I don't ask for a lot, Kate. I just want to make sure he's all right. I *need* to know. Consider it my dying declaration…"

I furrow my brow. "What's a dying declaration?"

"It just means it's the truth, is all. I want him to know the truth. I want him to know that what we had was real. I want him to know I loved him."

I squint my eyes and consider her. I don't know why she makes him out to be so important. But she does, and it makes me curious. "And returning the book will say all this?"

"Yes. And it will offer him closure. This way he won't spend the rest of his life wondering… He'll know if that book made it's way back to him, and I haven't—he'll know that he can let go. That was our deal."

"Okay," I agree. She doesn't believe me. I've agreed before. I've been pretty good at stalling, up until now. But considering what you said about offing her, and her desperation, I can see where she's coming from. She doesn't know it yet—

that I won't let anything happen to her. I have a plan for us. Other than you, she's the best friend I've ever had, and best friends are hard to come by in this line of work.

"Kate, I need you to understand something—really understand," she says. "That book was a gift. A very special gift. Returning it says everything."

"Fine," I relent. "I'll go." I don't tell her I'll do it as soon as tomorrow, but I will. That way the next time she asks I can surprise her.

She smiles as though she's read my mind. "Thank you," she says and it brightens up the whole room.

～

CHAPTER NINE

JUDE

You can't go to San Francisco with me. There's too much going on at home, or so you say. It isn't exactly a stretch, but mostly it's because of her. Also, you won't admit it, but you aren't sleeping. That makes two of us. The nightmares are back. I know because when you do drift off, it's fitful, and you mumble, and on occasion you even cry out. So, maybe you're right. Maybe it is better if you didn't come this time either. At least one of us will get more rest this way. That's not to say I don't miss the old days, the days we worked as a team. They weren't perfect; we had our issues. But at least we were together. Now, I'm not sure what we are. We're neither here nor there—or rather—you're here and I'm there.

I don't have a choice about leaving town. Otherwise, I lose time and money and eventually the mortgage doesn't get paid, and well, you know, it all goes down hill from there.

"I've been thinking—" you mention as you watch me pack, and this is how all bad conversations with women start, with them thinking. "That maybe it would be a good idea to have Brady talk to her."

And then you had to go and say that. And if I thought what you were going to say was going to suck, I hadn't known it would be this bad. "That's funny, Kate," I say running my fingers through my hair. "Really funny."

"Really?"

"No—not really. There's not a chance in hell," I tell you, and I can see that you're thinking what I won't know won't hurt me, but I can assure you, I will know.

"Hmm," you murmur, and I must have been right about what you were thinking, because you leave it at that.

I fold a pair of pants and place them in my bag. "Did you pick up the dry cleaning? I can't find my white shirt..."

Your expression tells me my answer. "Ummm."

"Damn it, Kate. You promised you would. That's my lucky shirt."

"Sorry," you offer but the way you say it, it's like you're not even listening. "You don't believe in luck," you add. "You're not even superstitious."

"I like that shirt."

You stand and walk around to the closet. I watch as you reach up to retrieve something from the shelf and as you do your skirt lifts slightly exposing your thigh, and that's all I needed. I'm going in, too. You turn and throw the shirt at me. It hits me in the face. "There, try that one. I said a good omen over it."

I brush the shirt away, letting it fall to the floor, and I look at you. You're a smart ass and I can't help myself. I lean back, grip the door handle and close the door behind me.

You squint. "Do we have time for this?"

"Yes," I say, lifting your shirt over your head. I check the time on my phone. My flight leaves in 90 minutes. That should do it. Your expression says you don't quite believe me, but what the hell, you need this as much as I do.

I slide your skirt over your hips and push you against the

wall. You part your legs and I like the way you open up for me. It's fast and it's heavy and sweaty and passionate, and I use you all the way up. It's everything I love about you, the way we fight without words.

"It's not, though," you say as you search the floor. You're looking for your shirt. I'm hoping it takes a while for you to find it.

"It's not what?"

"It's not funny."

You've lost me. "What's not funny?"

"Jesus. Do you even listen to anything I say?"

"It's Jude," I correct you. "And of course I listen."

"It's not funny that our son is hurting people. "

"Who said anything about it being funny?"

"I just don't know what to do about him," you say, pulling your shirt over your head. "You haven't seen the way those women look at me, Jude. The way they look at him—like he's some sort of monster."

"Who cares what they think?"

"Well, for starters, I do. I care!"

I don't know why I find this surprising. "What else is new?"

You cross your arms. "Stop!" you demand. "At some point, we're going to have to figure out a way to discuss things without arguing over semantics. We can't even get past that in order to fight about the important stuff."

"Fine," I tell you. And then, even though I don't want to, I add, "What do you want mc to say?"

"I don't know…that you'll take care of it. That you'll fix this."

I take you in my arms. I see what you want. "He's our son, Kate. Of course, I'll fix it. He just needs some discipline."

"I don't think that's what he needs," you sigh.

"Come with me, then. Bring the kids, if you want. Maybe we all just need a break from this place…"

"You know I can't," you reply, and I'm glad you say that, because I have work to do, and it doesn't entail lugging your drama along for the ride. "The kids need me here. They need stability."

"Yes," I agree, and I'm relieved, but I try not to let it show. It's hard to argue when you make such a good point.

"I think he needs an outlet. Someone to speak to…"

"No more third parties, Kate. We agreed."

I kiss your forehead and grab my bag. I'm late, and this conversation is headed nowhere good. "And no more trouble while I'm gone. Okay?"

"Of course not," you say. But you don't mean it, even though I can see that a part of you really wants to.

I MISS MY FLIGHT ON PURPOSE, BECAUSE I DON'T TRUST YOU. The case in California can wait, I decide. Of course, the fact that the plane took off without me makes my decision pretty easy. I check into a hotel downtown in order to take care of business on the home front. I have a few jobs here, as well. A lobbyist and one low-level criminal. Nothing out of the ordinary. Nothing exciting, and while it isn't exactly fair, it's why I hope you screw up. Not because I want to see you fail the test you aren't aware you're taking—but more so because if you're going to fail at all, I want to be around when it happens.

Better not to let a wound fester, that's what Rudy always says. He's concerned about you. He's called three times to say as much, and my father isn't much of a talker. Mostly, he's concerned about me. To be honest, I wouldn't put it past him to handle matters on his own. If he could kill his own wife, it certainly wouldn't be a stretch for him to dispose of mine. That's why he's first on my list to see. I need to pay him a visit; it's important he knows what he's up against. He isn't expecting me. It's better this way.

When he opens the door, I see it on his face. He knows this isn't one of those friendly father/son visits. But then, that's nothing new, we've never had those kind of visits anyhow.

"What's the occasion?" he asks, settling into his easy chair. I think about my mother way back when sitting in that same chair, her knees to her chest, rocking back and forth. I recall the fear in her eyes, how much she loved my father, how afraid she was, how she'd handled it all in the only way she knew how.

I move the newspaper off the couch so I have a place to sit. "I'm here about Kate."

"Surprise, surprise," he says, staring at the TV even though it's turned off. This is what his life has become, and I can't help but wonder what might have been, had he and my mother not been so toxic for one another. I think about the history here, and how I'll be damned if I let it repeat itself. He clears his throat. "It's always about a woman…"

I lean back on the couch, make myself comfortable. "Look —" I start and he does look, he stares straight at me. What I see in his eyes is disappointment, maybe a little regret, too. "I know you've never cared for her. But I do. I love her."

"Since when does what I think have to do with anything?"

"Since I was old enough to know better."

"That's the thing— I thought you did."

I don't know what to say to that, so I just sigh and study the ink on the newspaper. KILLER STRIKES AGAIN. I fold the paper, lean forward and stuff it in my back pocket.

"I don't think it's her," he says.

"What?"

"The article you just ripped off. It's not her."

I cock my head. "I didn't think it was."

"Well," he says, and he looks back at the TV. "Now that that's out of the way…"

"I need you to promise you're not going to do anything crazy…"

"I'm not the one you should be worried about."

"But I am worried—about you."

"She's going to take you down, Jude. I know you know that. What I don't know is why you refuse to do anything about it."

"Kate's not what you think."

"The hell she isn't!" he says, raising his voice. His face reddens. He takes a deep breath in and lets it out. I'm not sure I've ever seen my father this angry. "You didn't see what she did to that poor bastard the other night. He almost had her, from the looks of it. Which would make this conversation and your little visit pointless, now wouldn't it?"

"I've seen her work."

"That tells me everything I need to know…"

I lean forward, resting my elbows on my knees, and I stare at the floor.

"What are you going to tell those children when their mother winds up dead or in prison?"

I look up him. "The same thing you told me, I guess."

He doesn't meet my eye. He doesn't answer me for several minutes. In fact, I think he isn't going to, when he sucks in his lip. "That woman is a ticking time bomb. She's an open wound, she's infecting the rest of you, and if you don't remedy the situation she's going to do away with your whole family. Mark my words— it's just a matter of time. Sometimes you have to amputate. Let the leg go. Remove an arm. It's not easy—that decision—but you learn to deal. Trust me. Eventually, you learn. By God, do you learn. If it saves the rest of the body, you do what you gotta do. It's not a simple thing, knowing you have to kill someone you love. I'll be the first to tell you—there's nothing worse. But this isn't fairytale land we're living in, Jude. This is a dog-eat dog-world— eat or be eaten— kill or be killed. Sometimes people can find common ground. Sometimes not. You've tried, son. You have."

I stand. I refuse to listen to this for another second. He knows how close to home his words hit, and I think he wants it that way. "Yeah," I reply when I've settled on what I want to say. "Well, look how it turned out for you. You're alone in this empty house, and it's a fucking mess. Look at this place," I say, gesturing around. His eyes don't follow. They stay fixated on the floor. I run my fingers through my hair, pace the floor. "Look what you've become."

Eventually, when I've settled down he speaks. "Why'd you come?"

I take a deep breath in and let it out slowly. "I'm concerned that you might... come out of retirement."

He scoffs. "I did. The other night when you called."

"And I thanked you for that."

He cocks his head. "I think, from now on, you should leave me out of it. I want nothing to do with that woman and her antics."

"That woman is my wife."

He doesn't say anything, and he doesn't look at me for several long minutes. When he finally does, his expression is sullen, resigned. "And for that, I'm truly sorry. I can't save you from this one."

"I don't need you to save me. I just need you to say you won't hurt her."

"Don't you think if I'd wanted to do her harm, I would've?"

"I don't know," I reply, and it's the truth.

"It's probably better that way," he says. "Keeps you on your toes."

~

I DO THE ONLY THING THAT MAKES ANY SENSE AFTER MY VISIT with my father—I call Bob. We're in different time zones but he answers nonetheless. He always does.

"I'm failing," I tell him. "My father is right. I'm failing hard. I should be out of town, doing my job."

"Sometimes life is up and sometimes it's down," Bob tells me and his voice is sleepy.

"My life isn't just down—it's coming undone…I know what I'm supposed to do. Remove the threat. It's what I do—it's what I've always done."

"Then what's the problem?"

"It's her. I'm weak when it comes to her."

"Women tend to have that effect."

"Not on me."

"You called, didn't you?"

I sigh. "Rudy struck a nerve. You know how I hate being wrong. Now we aren't speaking, which makes judging his next move a little difficult…"

"Your dad has always been a level-headed man."

"Not when it comes to women."

"No," he says. "Not when it came to one."

"Speaking of one—you know the situation…with the therapist."

"You haven't dealt with that?"

I don't answer, which tells him what he needs to know.

"So, you've got double the trouble."

"Ever since that woman came into our lives—it's like she's gone off the deep end again. Ever since the little school incident with Brady, it only got worse."

"Brady is fine," Bob tells me. "You should send him over."

"I'm not my father…"

"Kids will be kids, Jude. What—would you rather him just let them pick on him? Would you rather he did nothing…"

"No. I probably should have handled it, though. Rather than putting it all on her."

"There's still time for that…"

"Yeah—" I agree. "Thanks for listening," I say.

"That's what I'm here for," he tells me, and the line goes dead. That's always been Bob's way of saying goodbye.

After the call, I feel better. But not well enough not to follow you. Rudy is right about one thing—you're the patient, and I'm the surgeon. Little do you know, we have an appointment. I realize it's time to see how bad this thing really is. I need to see for myself whether we can stand to merely keep an eye on it, or rather whether surgery is in order. I won't lie. I'd rather be anywhere but here. Watching — waiting— hoping—that I'm wrong. I grip the steering wheel and turn off behind you. I take a deep breath in, and I hold it. *Surprise me Kate; show me we can find middle ground.*

≈

I WATCH YOU IN THE DARK, AND IT FEELS LIKE OLD TIMES. YOU wait for him in an alley, and I've definitely seen you use this MO before. Which is how I know you know it's dangerous for women to be in dark alleys late at night. Also, I'd like to know, who is with our children?

I'm not ready to see how this ends. I'm not ready to save your life only to realize I have to take it. I text you.

Miss you. How are the kids?

You write back immediately: They're fine. Fast asleep. I'm headed that way too. Miss you. X

My stomach sinks. The fuck you are, and if lying to a

person is the same as missing them, then I don't know what kind of world this is you live in. Also, you're a better liar than I thought. You're quick. I decide to mess with you: You wanna FaceTime?

Once again, you don't skip a beat. You don't think about your response, you don't start to type and then backtrack, delete, delete, delete the way most people would. Nope. Not you. Your response is immediate. Confident. I kill the engine and read what you have to say: No I'm tired.

Well played. I write back: Ok. Goodnight. I love you.

My screen lights up: Love you.

God, Kate. I wish you weren't a liar.

But you are, which is why I sit watching you. It takes fifteen minutes or so, but eventually your company arrives. It doesn't escape me, the incongruity of my position. Most men would be sick over this, sick or livid, concerned their wives were up to no good, concerned they were having an affair. Not me. I'm worried that mine is just a plain ol' cold-blooded killer. It's a shame really, that I work so hard at this gig and get paid well for it, meanwhile you're willing to do it for free. Maybe that's the problem. Maybe that's why you're not more careful. You have no skin in the game.

I lean forward to get a closer look. You get out of the car. He's on foot. I watch as the two of you exchange a few words. I don't like the look of this guy. He glances around, from side to side, and then back at you. He's jittery. He's nervous, unsure in a way that makes him dangerous, and I swear if you let him get in that car with you, I might just kill the both of you here and now. Why wait and have to listen to your explanation? Better to get it over and done with, I say.

Only you don't let him get in your car. You reach into your waistband, and you take him out execution style. The poor bastard doesn't even see it coming. You tick every box, just right—from the way you handle him— to the way you make your getaway. *Good girl.* You make me proud, even though I want to be mad. If I weren't supposed to be in a different state, I'd drive home and show you just how good you are. It does things to me, Kate, seeing you like this. Knowing you're capable, that you can handle your own. I needed to see for myself that you've got this. Mission accomplished. It's dangerous and exciting and, quite frankly, fucking crazy. Sure, my father is right about one thing, but it's not the thing he thinks. I could have married a nice girl, one who I could depend on to raise my kids up right and have a home-cooked meal on the table when I came home. But I didn't. I picked you. Maybe I'm all the worse for it, but it's too late to stop now. I don't think I could if I tried. I need to see you. Now. I need to show you what I feel.

~

I TAKE CARE OF THE LOBBYIST, WAIT THREE HOURS, AND THEN check out of the hotel and head home. The other job can wait. I've got you to take care of. When I arrive home, I'm glad you're not sleeping. It's not surprising that you're up there in that room, which is actually a good thing, because I manage to surprise the both of you.

Your eyes grow wide when you see me punch in the code. You glare at her and narrow your focus.

I glance around the small room. It appears the two of you are having some kind of slumber party and it's fucking ridiculous— but at least you're home safe and sound. There's a part of me that wants a fight, that wants to demand to know what you're doing here—what your plan is— how you see this all turning out. But then there's the other part of me who had a long day, who is proud of what I witnessed—the way you handled that kill— and so I simply kiss your forehead and ask how your night was instead. I'm not a fan of concession, and I hope for both our sake, you see it for what it is: a diversion—a delay tactic—a chance to consider my next move. A chance to let you dig yourself in a little deeper, if that's what you wanna do.

"Good," you say, but I can see it in your eyes. You're concerned. "Why are you home?"

I wince just slightly. "I couldn't stand to be away."

"That's not like you," you say, and you shift and then scoot up to a sitting position. You wait for me to say more, but I don't. I won't. Eventually, you stand and lead me out of that room. You've proven not once but twice tonight that you can do the right thing, and it makes me happy.

"I'm glad to see you, too," I joke. But you apparently aren't in a joking mood. You look away.

I don't think you're going to respond, but then you do. "I'm surprised you were able to get a flight this late."

I run my fingers up your arm. "I caught the red eye."

You study my face like there's something on your mind. But you're quiet as you climb into bed and watch me undress. "Come here," you say, patting the empty space beside you, and eventually, I do.

～

CHAPTER TEN

KATE

You snore all night long. Meanwhile, I lie there in the dark, plotting revenge. I guess it's fine that you're back early. At least I got an orgasm out of the deal. On the flip side, you're lying to me, and I'm not sure why. I checked, there weren't any direct flights and you refuse to fly on any airline but one. So either you weren't really in San Francisco, or you never really left.

Maybe you can see that I know you're a liar, and maybe that's why this morning you're up early making pancakes and helping to get the kids off to school. I would've sworn it was all guilt, but then you go and open your mouth and we get a little closer to the truth. "I have to leave again," you say nonchalantly.

You're perched in the doorway of the utility room, watching me move a load of laundry from the washer to the dryer.

I look up at you. "Well, that explains it."

Your eyes are set. You aren't looking for a fight, but you're worried you've found one. "Explains what?"

"Everything."

133

"Stop," you say, and you nod at the basket. "Why don't you let Rosa handle that? It's what we pay her for."

"Laundry helps me think. Also, Cheryl says performing routine tasks helps people process their feelings. "

"Huh," you say, and you look a bit alarmed, probably because you're a man, and men don't like talking about feelings. "I guess we don't need Rosa anymore then."

I roll my eyes.

You try another route in. "What's got you thinkin' so hard this morning?"

"Nothing."

You rest your arm against the doorframe, making sure to take up the entire space—making sure I couldn't get by even if I wanted to. "It's *not* nothing. Just spit it out."

I raise my brow. "No, really. Never mind."

You take a step forward, and it seems like the walls come with you. This room feels so small with you in it. "So, you aren't mad I have to go?"

"Of course not. It's your job—you have to do what you have to do, right?"

You look surprised, and I like it when I have this effect on you. You take another step forward, closing in. You fold your lips, cornering me. You force me back until my hips are pressed against the washing machine.

"Not again," I say as you press your mouth to my neck. "I have things to do."

You hit the spot, the one you know so well. "So do I."

You wrap your hand around my throat and squeeze lightly. I have to admit that your intensity, your enthusiasm, it turns me on. Still, I have other things on my mind and so I shift.

"Jude," I sigh. "Seriously."

"This is serious," you say, and you smile. "I could kill you if I wanted to."

"Maybe you are."

Your mouth falls open. "Are you going to tell me what's wrong? Or not."

I force out all the air in my lungs. You let your hand fall against my hip. I want to tell you it's because you're a liar. But first— I want to find out why you lied to begin with. You're hiding something, and I need to know what that something is. Also, you're not helping, where our son is concerned. My life is falling apart.

You furrow your brow. "I guess not, then?"

"It's nothing," I tell you.

"You're going to have to let this nothing thing go…"

I roll my neck. "Yeah."

"Let. It. Go," you whisper, your breath hot against my ear. I try, I really, really do. You slip your hand inside my draw-string pants, and I have to say, it helps. "I have an idea…" you say.

I swallow hard. I like your idea. It offsets the anger problem. "Really?"

"Let me help you forget," you shush me, reading my mind, releasing the string. I watch it slip through your fingers, and any resolve I have slips right along with it. And that's that. Next thing I know, I'm on the washer, you're between my legs, and we're holding onto one another, pushing and pulling, doing what we do best. Fighting without words. Trying to salvage something neither of us is sure is broken.

∼

I TAKE HER COFFEE IN AND SIT DOWN AND SIP MY OWN. IT'S MY second cup. Today seems to call for it. "I never thought I'd say this," I say to her. "But as I watched him back out of the drive, it was good to see him go. I feel like I can finally breathe…"

She stares at her book, looking up only briefly to let me know she's listening.

"He's just so needy lately. It's like I don't even know who he is anymore…"

"How so?"

"I don't know," I say. "But when he told me there was another trip, all I know is that I wasn't angry like I normally would be. All I felt was relief."

"That's called growth, Kate."

"Yes, well, that's not what it felt like last night. Not at all. You saw, I was freaking out when he showed up here unannounced."

"This is his home. I'd hardly say he just showed up."

"You know what I mean…I just didn't want to have to lie."

"About?"

"I didn't want to tell him I'm back at it. I promised I'd stay out of trouble. Especially while he's away. Had he come home any sooner, I would've been busted, and I couldn't let that happen. Suddenly, all of my lies were stacked like dominos, and I couldn't have everything coming down at once…"

"Why not just tell the truth then? What's so wrong with the truth?"

"I don't want him worrying about things here while he's away. You know how that is—what this line of work calls for. Anyway—" I say, ready to change the subject. "I've got it handled. It's important he sees that."

"Hmmm— Maybe the person you're not being honest with in all of this is yourself."

"Maybe," I sigh. "I just have to be more careful from now on."

"You seem irritated at my suggestion," she tells me, and I hate it when she does this, when she points out the obvious. "I didn't get what I needed last night…"

"You never finished telling me what happened."

"What happened is… I went to that alley with a purpose, and it all turned to shit. I went there to get even, to get my fill, hoping to sort out my thoughts. I went there to feel what I needed to feel."

"But what's the point of it all? Why are you doing it?"

"Ummm…Well…I figure if I can catch the killer, then they'll see. They'll know I'm more than just a mom, more than just someone's wife. Instead, what happened was the guy found me out."

"What guy?"

"Good Cat—" I laugh.

She looks at me sideways.

"That was his name on the hookup site. I know. It's as crazy as it sounds," I tell her and she narrows her gaze. "People are so weird online—no one is who they say they are and nothing is as it seems. *Good Cat,*" I repeat. "Give me a break. Anyway—he said he wanted someone to be his kitten. I shit you not—that's what he wrote. He said it would be fun; he said that he would take care of me, and I didn't disagree. Turns out—you shouldn't believe everything you read on the internet. I thought I would teach *him* a lesson. But it turned out, he did most of the teaching."

"And—what'd you learn?"

"I learned it wasn't going to turn out the way I wanted," I scoff. She waits patiently.

I shake my head. "How was I supposed to know he was one of those hacker types?"

"Oh," she says. She smiles and I can see that she's amused despite how hard she tries to hide it.

"Yeah—he told me that he knew who I was, he said he saw me for what I am. He said that I seemed like a nice lady, and I shouldn't be doing what I'm doing. For a minute I thought maybe I'd been *really* found out, but then I realized—no. He just meant advertising myself online for sex with strange men. He wanted me to know I'm too good for that. He said I need to find God. And if not God, then something that fulfills me. He insisted I don't know my own worth, and that's when it hit me. This does fulfill me. Killing: the thrill of not getting caught; knowing that I'm doing something worthwhile; cleaning up the streets of our hometown. Trying to find the bastard who's preying on women, killing them all because they like sex with strangers. That's my destiny. That is the kind of thing I'm meant for. I know Jude would be proud, too, if only I could tell him the truth. Which—obviously—I can't."

"I see."

"Anyway, it sucked, especially after my little revelation. Basically, having to shoot him point-blank. I took it right out of my husband's playbook. One and done. It's too bad," I lament. I sip my coffee, and I contemplate whether or not to go on. Eventually, I do. "I wanted to have a little fun. I wanted to teach him that women aren't playthings to be discarded whenever one has gotten their fill. I wanted to show him the error of his ways—preferably slowly and painfully. Instead, I was wrong about him. He wasn't a bad guy *per se*, but he was a liar, so there's that. A liar who taught me to be more careful."

"So you learned something. Where's the harm in that?"

I cock my head. *Has she not heard anything I've just said?* I exhale loudly. "If only he hadn't been so nosy. Curiosity killed the cat, I said to him…"

"But why'd you do it? After you knew he wasn't who he made himself out to be?"

I shrug. "I couldn't help it. He looked at me, really looked at me, and that's when I saw it."

She furrows her brow. "You saw what?"

"That thing in his eyes. The thing that lets me know. It told me he was going to be trouble. In fact, he already was. It was like I could see the future, and it ended with him turning up at my doorstep like a stray trying to help me find God, or my worth, or something that was never missing in the first place. He made me remember who I really am, and that's when I knew I had to make him forget." I shrug. "Shooting him in the head seemed like as good a solution as any."

～

SHE DIDN'T OUTRIGHT SAY SO, BUT I KNOW MY STORY MADE her happy. I think I'm onto something here. She wants me to feel things, and this, I can feel. I'm thinking I need to do something special for her. I'm thinking about my next kill, and when I might have time for it. That's the thing I was angry with you about earlier, well, that, and your lies. You have your work, and I'm glad. But where does that leave me? I'll tell you. It leaves me with everything else. And it turns out, everything else is a lot. I'm all over the place. It's not the way it used to be—killing, I mean—not now that I have a family. Not with the kids in school, and life being so hectic, not with you being gone so much. Carving out time for myself is like pulling teeth. That's why I'm not happy. Something has to give, and that something can't always be me. I need an outlet. I need more than either you or her can offer. I need to be me again. If I want to find this killer, if I want to settle the score, then I'm going to have to find a sitter, and one I can trust. I'm not sure I should ask Josie again. I'm contemplating calling her when the phone rings. I see the number flash on the screen. It's the school, and I can feel it isn't good.

"Mrs. Riley?" the principal asks.

"Yes?"

She inhales. "There's been another incident with Brady. A very serious incident."

I hold my breath.

"He's fine," she says next. "But I feel the rest would be best discussed in person. How soon can you get here?"

I already know the answer. Four minutes and seven seconds. I don't tell her that, however. Instead I tell her I'm on my way.

I rush into the office, like the hot mess I am, completely and utterly unsure of what I'm going to run into this time. The clerk asks me to have a seat, and I do. I see her pick up the phone and whisper into the receiver, and my stomach sinks further, if that's even possible. It's like I'm on a carnival ride, the kind that bounces up and down, and you never know whether the next time is the last.

"She'll be with you in a moment," the clerk informs me. I shift in my seat. It's one of those uncomfortable chairs, the kind that feels awful, as though the whole world and everyone in it knows. They glare at you, pity upon their faces, the understanding that your kid is a troublemaker, that you're a failure as a mother. They smile, but it isn't a real smile. It's just their way of saying they're thankful. Better you than them to get stuck with *that kind* of child.

Another woman, one I don't recognize, calls my name, and I look up. "This way," she says, motioning for me to follow. We walk down a long hallway, one I've been down before. It feels different to be here for reasons other than volunteering, to be on the other end of things. She stops at the principal's door and motions for me to go in. I don't want to. I just stand there for a moment, paralyzed, until she clears her throat, and I know I can't hold out forever.

The principal looks up from her desk as I make my way in. She offers me a seat, and when she speaks she sounds tired, the way I feel. I watch closely for clues as she leans across the desk and then settles back in her chair. There aren't any, but I can tell she's not sure where to start.

"Thank you for coming Mrs. Riley," she says. "I'll call Brady in momentarily, but I wanted the opportunity to speak with you alone before doing so."

I wait for it. She looks away and then back at me.

She presses her lips together. "Brady started a fire in our tool shed this morning."

I keep my expression neutral. It isn't easy. "He did what?"

"The fire department was called and a report was filed with the police."

I tilt my head "Why would he do that? *How* would he do that?"

"I wish I could tell you," she says, wetting her lips. "But once again he is refusing to speak."

"Where is he?" I ask, standing. I need to see him, and it needs to happen now.

She looks toward the door. "He's in the nurse's office."

"Why is he there?"

She scoots out from under her desk and pushes her chair back. "I'm going to walk you down there..." she says, standing.

Next thing I know I'm following her down another long hall.

"Brady," she calls, opening the door to a darkened room. "Your mom is here."

I see Brady sit up, and already I can see the indifference in his expression. He looks exactly like you sitting there. Only different, because *his eye is swollen and there's dried blood under his nose.* I turn to the principal. My voice raises. "What the hell happened here? Why is my son's face bruised?"

"Brady and Jackson were in an altercation," she says, looking at me directly. She stands up a little straighter. "I'll leave it to him to explain."

I glare at her, as though to ask if she's kidding me. "I think you need a moment to calm down. Talk to your son," she tells me with a nod. I say nothing as she closes the door, but in my mind she's on the floor, with my hands around her neck. I know I have to be careful. My palms are sweaty, and my heart is racing, and Brady is watching. She opens it again briefly, peeking her head in. "Oh—and I'd like to see you back in my office after the two of you have gotten the chance to talk."

I turn away toward Brady. She closes the door.

"They hit me, mom," he says. He doesn't wait for me to ask, he just says it.

I wipe my hands on my jeans. "Who hit you?"

"Those boys."

I swallow hard. I can hear blood pulsing in my ears, my face growing hot, and I know I have to get out of there before I do something I regret.

I gather Brady up, and I ask the office clerk to call Olivia from her classroom. I wait out in the hall. When I see her coming around the corner, looking so little, I almost cry. She looks at Brady and grabs his hand.

"They hurt you again," she says and tears do come. I brush them away, and I take them home. We need to regroup. And I desperately need to talk to you.

LATER OLIVIA REMINDS ME SHE HAS BALLET. I'M STILL TRYING to get a hold of you, and I'd been so distracted by everything that I'd forgotten today is Tuesday. *Dance day.* She's already mad at me for pulling her out of school. Apparently, I made her miss reward day, and I don't want to feel the wrath over messing up dance as well. So I take Brady to your father's, figuring maybe a little male bonding will do him good after the day he's had. Of course, I drop him at the curb because your father hates me, and asking him to babysit was the last thing I wanted to have to do.

"Tell your grandpa the truth," I say, and he nods. I doubt he'll say anything at all, and for a moment I feel sadness so extreme I have to pull the car over.

"Let's go," Olivia chides from the backseat. "We're going to be late."

I swallow my feelings, my words, everything. I stuff it down until it's safe to let it out.

Halfway between your father's place and dance class, Olivia calls my name. Twice. "Brady told me a secret… do you wanna hear?"

"Sure," I say. But I'm lost in thoughts of my own. I'm thinking about what we're going to have for dinner, you, and the committee meeting I'm supposed to hold at the school tomorrow, the one I never want to show my face at again, and so while I'm listening, and I respond, I don't really hear what she's saying.

"Brady told me he hears things. He told me not to tell anybody…he says it makes him do bad things," she pipes up, speaking louder, and she has my full attention now.

"What kind of bad things?" I ask, glancing at her in the rearview mirror.

"I don't know. He didn't tell me that part."

I look up and realize the car in front of me has stopped. I brake hard. The tires squeal. My hands grip the wheel so tightly, my knuckles turn white.

"Sorry, Mommy," Olivia says once we've come to a full stop, and I catch my breath.

"It's not your fault," I tell her. "I wasn't paying attention."

Traffic starts to move again, and eventually I loosen my grip.

She exhales and I hear the concern in it. "You don't think he'd do bad things to me, do you?"

My stomach turns. "No, of course not," I say. "Your brother loves you…"

"Yeah, that's what he says when he wants me to play with him. But I don't believe him."

"Brady loves you, Liv."

I watch her eyes in the mirror.

She shrugs, and a lump forms in my throat. I hold my breath pretty much for the remainder of the evening. I don't let it out, not really, not until I've spoken to her. She always knows exactly the right thing to say.

~

I'M PANICKING AND PACING THE SMALL ROOM. CHERYL watches. "Jude is going to make us move. I know it. After everything with Brady—given the fact that there's a police report. It's just too risky. We can't stay here…"

"So you move."

"Yeah," I tell her. "You're right— at this point that's sort of the least of my problems."

She watches me closely as I pinch the bridge of my nose. "And I told him…I TOLD HIIM not to take my kids shooting."

"Shooting?"

"Jude's father. When I picked Brady up tonight, he told me he'd gone shooting. Why on earth he would think that's what Brady needs right now, I haven't a clue. I mean, after everything we've been through in the last few weeks… Not to mention the fire…"

"You need to calm down. Sit," she tells me, and I do.

"I have no doubt his grandfather taught him well—he thinks my kids need the same kind of training their father had— when that's the last thing they need. To turn out like us…. Seriously? Target practice—I mean, it's like why not

144

give him something else to add to his repertoire. I guess arson wasn't good enough."

I don't know why she tells me what she does. Maybe it's good old-fashioned self-preservation, maybe she's just trying to make me feel better. "But why would Brady start a fire?"

I shake my head. "Why does Brady do anything? He doesn't sleep, he hardly talks…I don't know. I don't know what to do to get through to him. Same as his father in a lot of ways…"

"Did you ask him about the bruises?"

"He said kids were making fun of him. He said they hit him—I mean, that much is obvious. But was a fire the answer? "

"You need to put more pressure on the school to find out what's really going on. If you ask me, the fire was a cry for help."

"A cry for help?"

"Doesn't he have a history of doing stuff like this? Out of retaliation?"

I think back to the babysitter and the way she looked laying at the bottom of the stairs, and I try to recall if I've ever told her this. Eventually, I sort of shrug.

"Maybe you're missing the forest for the trees," she says, and it annoys me when she does this. I hate it when people say maybe when it's clear they don't mean it. She has her professional hat on, and suddenly it's all therapist speak. *Where's a friend when you need one?*

"Maybe," I tell her.

"If you ask me—"

"Have I?"

"You're holding me hostage in a room in your home and you're pacing back and forth like a mad woman— so I'd say so."

I roll my eyes. I hate it when she pretends she doesn't like it here.

"Anyway, could it be possible that you're missing the whole point?"

"What point am I missing?"

"You think your purpose is out there tracking down a killer, when really your purpose needs to be here at home focusing on the one you have in the making."

I swallow hard, and I have to get out of this room before I do something I regret. I need to speak to you. I make a move toward the door. Her words stop me in my tracks. "Sometimes you're too close to the story to see the truth of it. Sometimes you need to step back, gain some distance, get a little perspective," she says, and I almost listen.

～

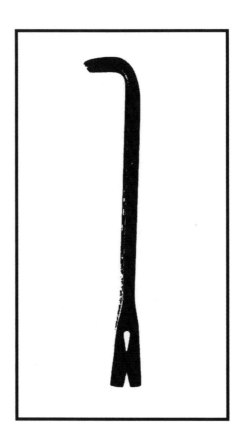

CHAPTER ELEVEN

JUDE

I make it to the airport, but I never do catch my flight. Last thing I remember is turning off the engine and opening the car door— after that things seem to get a bit hazy. I guess that tends to happen when one is hit in the head, bound, gagged, and drugged. Next thing I know, when I come to again, I'm alone in some old house. It smells like old books and after-shave.

"Oh, good. You're awake," a male voice calls from the shadows. He's been watching me, obviously. *Waiting*.

I don't answer, because the best way to learn anything is to shut up and listen. There's also the fact that I'm not dead yet, which tells me he wants something.

"You have information I want," he says, and this is good, it appears we're in sync. Still, I say nothing. Even if I wanted to speak to this bastard, my mouth is dry and stuffed with cloth of some kind, and in any case, I don't. It isn't the pounding headache that bothers me most, or even the fact that I'm likely never going to see you or my kids again, but the blood, which drips down my forehead and into my eyelashes. I think it has to be one of the worst feelings there is, the maddening feeling of something moving across your face slowly, when there's not much you can do about it. In this case, I can't. Not with my hands tied behind my back.

"You want water?" he asks, and I do, but I'm not going to ask for it. My decision was made the moment I regained consciousness. And truth be told, long before that. Bob trained me for this scenario all those years ago, back when I was a kid. I never forgot what I learned. Which is why I refuse to cooperate with anything he asks, and I'm sure as hell not going to give in for small comforts. I bring my shoulder up toward my face and do my best to brush the blood away. I think about you and the kids. And then I force myself to shake the thought away. Getting emotional won't help me now. Finding oneself in this situation—for someone in my line of work—is always a possibility. So I'm not shocked to be in this position—but that doesn't mean I'm okay with it either. At any rate, if this guy wanted me dead I would be, which lets me know that whatever comes next isn't going to be pleasant.

∼

"Mr. Riley," he says, jabbing the needle into my vein. I only see his feet; it's too dark to see much else. Also, my eyes are nearly swollen shut. I do make out that he's wearing nice leather loafers, strange, if you ask me, for someone in his line of work. "If you aren't going to talk, then I see no point in keeping you awake. Rest well," he says and he makes a clucking sound with his mouth. "I've got all the time in the world. You, however, have about three days before your body begins shutting down without water. Don't worry though—it won't always be this easy. The drugs will wear off, and so will my generosity, and before long there'll be nothing ahead of you but long hours in the dark. Suit yourself," he advises. "Do what you need to do."

I recall my training. *Hold out. Just hold out. It's hard to hold out when you lose consciousness.* As I drift further into the darkness, I try to remember the last meal I ate. My memory is fuzzy and anyway all I can think of is you.

I don't know how long I'm out for. Maybe hours, maybe a whole day. Maybe more. What I do know is that when I wake I have to piss. I also know that if I ask permission, it's setting a tone. One I refuse to set. In the end, I piss myself.

❧

"MY GOD, IT REEKS IN HERE," HE SAYS. THE ROOM IS LIT NOW, and I can see that the chains around me are connected to a bedpost in the middle of a bedroom. Whoever this guy is, he seems run of the mill, not at all prepared to keep a captive. But he does have good drugs, I'll give him that. That's the thing about crazy people. You can never quite gauge the exact level of crazy. Why he's keeping me here, in a spare bedroom, I have no idea. What I do realize is that given my surroundings, it's a temporary solution for what he likely sees as a temporary problem. Otherwise, he'd have a more elaborate setup.

I blink, or squint really—the light kills my eyes. It's still hard to see but when a hand reaches toward my face, I flinch, even though I wish I hadn't. It's instinctive. He pulls the gag from my mouth, and I take a deep breath in and exhale as fast as I can. I look up, but all I see is light pouring in, killing my head, and so I shut my eyes again. It isn't easy; I have to force myself. Fear will do that to a person. The last thing you want to do in a situation like this is to lose one of your senses.

He walks away, and I steady my breath. It's important that

I focus. I'm not cooperating—but I'm not ready to die yet either. Eventually, I open my eyes, and my vision adjusts. That's when I see there's a window. *A way out.* It has curtains and blackout shades but that's not where the light comes from. I follow the shadows to where the man with the leather loafers sits. He's in an old wooden rocker next to a table with a lamp on it. I pull at the chain. Not to see if it's long enough to reach him, I already know it isn't, but it's uncomfortable against my wrists, he has the cuffs too tight.

"You have something I want," he says.

I swallow, and I meet his eye. His silhouette is still blurry; what I have is a concussion, if I'm lucky. If not, it's the drugs, or something more serious, something I don't want to think about. From what I'm able to make out, he's older than I figured he'd be. Tall and lanky, with well-educated eyes, and a face that's seen a lot. This isn't good news, I know, him letting me see his face. I realize he wants me alive, for now, just long enough to get what he wants. But if he'd intended to let me go, he'd have made sure I never got a good look at him. Guys like me don't let this sort of thing go. Which only means one thing. One of us is going to die.

He sighs long and slow. "We need to get you cleaned up. I can't have my house smelling like a rest home."

I want to tell him it smells like mothballs and rotting paper, and ugliness; I want to tell him the piss only adds to the ambiance of the place, but I don't.

"I'm going to unlock your cuffs," he says, throwing a pair of sweatpants in my direction. "I assume you're all good with elimination?"

I don't take my eyes off his.

"Well," he says when I don't answer. "It certainly smells like you managed well."

I follow his gaze as he nods in the direction of a bucket. "For next time," he says, and he walks over to me. I study the shadow of the pistol in his hand as he unlocks my cuffs, just as he said he would. He scoots the sweatpants in my direction with the toe of his shoe and backs away. Once my hands are free, I rub at my wrists and then I use the bed to pull myself to a standing position. I'm doing it to test my strength, but it's useless. My legs are mostly numb. As I shake them out, I look up at him. I can't have been out too long, not if I'm able to stand. His eyes narrow, and he steadies the gun on me. He motions for me to get a move on. I unbutton my jeans and wiggle out of them but I don't take my eyes from his. I may be weak, but I won't back down. That's when the smell of old piss hits me, and it jars something in me. Hobbling on one leg, I slide the jeans off and pick up the sweatpants. I shake them out and put them on, one foot, and then the other before sliding them up over my hips. When I'm finished, I roll my neck, and that's when I make my move. I bum rush the guy, only he fires, and I take a bullet.

"Motherfucker!" I cry out, and I fall on my ass, gripping my foot. The pain prevents me from making another move, the burning searing through any ambition I once had.

"I was afraid you might try that," he tells me making a hissing noise. Then he jabs a needle straight in my neck.

～

"YOUR WIFE IS WORRIED ABOUT YOU. THAT'S THE BAD NEWS," he tells me, and *motherfucker* I knew this was bound to happen. I just hoped I'd have more time. "The good news is, she was very helpful on the phone."

I look down at my foot. It's bandaged, expertly so, and it crosses my mind that maybe this guy is a physician. Whatever he is, he's certainly not a novice. I wiggle my toes and I feel faint. I can see blood is starting to seep through the bandages.

"All I wanted was to know what you did with her… You made it so difficult…but it turned out you weren't the person with answers at all."

I cock my head.

"You wasted my time," he huffs.

I stare at my foot and I wonder how bad it is. I feel numb. "I thought about amputating," he says and he laughs. I wiggle my toes.

"Get up," he orders, gripping me underneath my arm. "We're going to pay your wife a visit. It'll be unexpected. Which is to say—not my favorite kind. I prefer manners over convenience, personally. But surely she'll be glad to see you one last time."

Damn it Kate. Why? Why would you talk to him? Why?

He reads my mind. "She paid me a visit, you know. That wife of yours. She's really something. That's what led me to you…so in a way, you have her to thank for all this…"

I exhale. He notices.

"Stand up," he demands again, this time pulling on my arm. "Once you're in the car, a little more of this," he says showing me the syringe. "Just enough to take the edge off."

I think. Really think. I need a plan, and whatever it is, it can't be letting this bastard anywhere near that house.

"Don't worry," he tells me, reading my mind once again. *He's good.* I'll give him that. "She's going to know you're a killer. Just like I know her husband paid you to take care of her."

I don't know what he's talking about. It hurts to breathe. I'm inhaling and exhaling rapidly like a woman in labor and it isn't pretty. It hurts to move. It hurts to think.

"Oh, now you're the one who is confused. Wonderful," he says as I stagger. He helps me down a long hallway. "Since we've got a bit of time on our hands, let me explain…" I drop to the floor because I just can't stand any longer. Not on one foot, and certainly not on both. He orders me to crawl, and I do, all the while considering my options.

"You took something from me… Now it's your time to see what that feels like." He nudges me with his foot. "I've been racking my brain, trying to come up with how to get retribution. What qualifies as equality when you take something so precious from a person…there's a question for you."

I pause, unable and unwilling to continue. "What do you think, Jude? An eye for an eye? A lover for a lover?" he asks, and I know I can't let him get me in that car. At the same time, it doesn't matter; it seems he wants to pay you a visit, and if that's the case, I'd rather be alive to see it.

"But not to worry, my boy, I've figured it out. I want that motherfucker of a husband of hers," he laughs. I don't understand what's funny. "But you'll do for now."

"Move," he says nudging my injured foot with the tip of his shoe and as soon as the pain subsides just a little, I crawl on. "I knew she didn't just run off with him. I knew she wouldn't leave like that. And I've been looking, you know. I never would've stopped. Thankfully that sweet little wife of yours stepped in and saved the day. She helped me see what retribution looks like— and it all starts with you."

"She isn't sweet," I say, and if he's going to hear anything from me, it's that. *Also, fuck.*

"He speaks."

I stop there with the talking, but I keep moving. Or at least I think I do. I'm already drowsy, fuzzy, barely conscious. I'm considering what I can do to keep him from injecting me with anything else. I need to be alert for what comes next. And dear God, Kate, if there ever was a time for you to shirk your motherhood duties off on Josie, please let that time be now.

We make it to the garage, and he clears his throat. He likes to talk, this one. "Here's the thing, Jude," he says popping the trunk. "I have no skin in the game, here. I couldn't care less whether you see your wife again. Make a move—you're dead. As for me, I'll be paying her a visit regardless…"

He puts me in the trunk. *So this is what this feels like.* "Rest easy," he says, shutting it in my face.

He drives. I wiggle and shift and roll over, and eventually he slams on the brakes. "I'm no moron Mr. Riley. I've seen enough movies to know how this goes down. I just hope you have, too."

I've seen a few. But that's not why I do what I do. I'm too drugged up to think that clearly anyhow. My hands are handcuffed but I shift enough so that I can fiddle with the taillights. I manage to disable one of them. I'm fishing for the emergency latch when I feel the car slow, and pull to the right. Eventually, it comes to a complete stop. I hear the driver's door open and I take my position. As he lifts the trunk, I use both feet to kick up at him as hard as I can. It's of little use. I see what's in his hand. The tire iron comes down on my skull. One and done.

≈

MAYBE I'M DEAD. MAYBE I'M NOT. AT THIS POINT, IT'S HARD to say. Maybe he hasn't just clubbed me in the trunk of his car. Maybe this is all a dream. If so, I want to wake up now. "This is what happens when you take everything from a man, Jude. You'll see."

I can hear him tearing a needle from its wrapper. I'm still in the trunk, but I have no idea how much time has passed. My hearing is acute enough that I can hear the liquid being sucked from the vial into the syringe. That's what happens when your eyes stop working. "The book," he mutters. "I thank God for that book."

My mouth fills with blood, and I spit so I don't choke. I hunch forward just as much as I can, which isn't much and I dry heave into the thin, scratchy carpeting, and that's how I know I'm not dead. Death couldn't possibly be this uncomfortable. I hear him pause to take me in. "You're not dead yet," he says and I can't think, I can't focus, but I swear he's no run-of-the-mill killer. This guy is good. He either knows what he's doing or he really has lost everything. People, as a general rule, aren't this ruthless unless they're out of options.

"Your wife thought she was doing the right thing by returning it—but I can't help but think it's all karma. She wanted me to find you; she did."

He laughs. "She talked about ending your relationship, you know. I get it now. It's gotta be hard living with someone like you. You're a low life nobody—that's what you are. She just can't bring herself to leave because you provide a roof over her head and some facade of the perfect little life. But don't kid yourself—she isn't staying because she wants to. She stays for two reasons: one—she's afraid for her life. And she should be. Two, and maybe this is even worse—she fears she can't get anything better. What a pity that is—that she'll turn out to be right on both fronts."

He injects me with his poison, and slowly at first, and then all of a sudden, I fall into the darkness again.

Minutes, or hours later, who knows, I hear him humming to the radio. We drive on. Every once in a while he pauses, turns down the radio, and calls to me, "You okay back there?"

I don't answer. My head is swimming. Also, I have nothing to say.

He sighs and turns down the radio, and then he brakes hard. "No worries," he calls. "We're almost there." I shift my position, testing to see how far I can go. Not far.

"Glad you're up," he says. "Honestly, the drugs make this

whole thing less fun. Numbing yourself out is never the answer, you know."

I cough, and I taste metal. I spit blood.

"It's funny. When you're having an affair with a hitman's wife—well—you know something like this is bound to happen sooner or later. Men like him aren't just gonna let it slide when you shag and snag their woman. No. Men like that are going to extinguish the threat. And yet—that's not what he did at all. Turned out he was smarter than that. I guess, he showed the both of us in the end, didn't he? He took her from me. He killed her. That or he hired you to do it—and either way I get the sense that you're not going to say which it is. But that piece of truth is irrelevant. It doesn't matter… I'll find him eventually. Come to think of it—that's probably something you can help with…"

He turns up the radio again, appears to change his mind, and turns it off. "That's the irony of it all, you see. She was going to hire you to kill *him*. It was our little plan. It never got that far though, did it? He got to you first," he says, and the car slows. He lets out a small laugh. "But I got to you last."

Shag and snag. Shag and snag. I repeat those words over and over in my mind. Anything to keep from losing consciousness again.

It works, because the next thing I know I'm being dragged up my walk to the side entrance of our home.

"Unlock the door," he says, which is pointless. He's mocking me because he knows I can't. I watch as he does it instead.

$\sim$

YOU'RE IN THE KITCHEN PUTTING UP DISHES.

"Oh good," you say but you don't turn around. "You're home."

"Kate," I call but your name comes out garbled. It reverberates in my ears, and I'm not sure I've said anything at all. You turn.

"Kate," he copies. He aims a gun at you. "How lovely to see you again…"

Your eyes grow wide, and I realize then that you weren't expecting us. You take in my condition and you frown. I watch as you carefully set the dishtowel you were holding aside.

You shake your head. "So that's *why* you didn't answer your phone…"

"Sit down," he orders but you don't make a move. I see you take a butcher knife from the dishwasher. He sees, too.

"Set that down," he says, pistol-whipping me. "And then sit your ass in that seat."

This time you do as you're told.

"Your husband has taken something from me."

"Is this about the book?" you ask, and I think you're going to tell him about her, and you shouldn't. I hope you can read this in my expression. You don't.

"No," he tells you. "I just thought I could help you come to a decision on your relationship issues…"

"This seems like a lot of trouble to go to," you say, and *what the fuck is wrong with you*, using sarcasm at a time like this.

He smirks, and he leans back against the door. "No trouble at all."

≈

CHAPTER TWELVE

KATE

"I've been trying to get a hold of you," I say, standing to put on water for tea. "You know I hate it when you don't answer my calls." I don't ask our visitor permission to make a drink—this is my home, and I'll do what I damned well please. Plus, I get the feeling this might take a while. He doesn't say anything—he doesn't tell me to sit back down; he simply watches my every move. I can see in his eyes, uncertainty, and I get the sense he's beginning to realize this is all a little more than he bargained for.

You, too, are watching my every move as I fill the kettle. I feel your eyes on me, they're asking a million unspoken questions, questions I don't yet have all the answers to. I turn on the burner, lean down to eye level, and study the flame. Then I look back at you. I'm not sure you understand anything I've just said because you're looking at me like I've lost my mind. I haven't. Not yet. Of course, you're not thinking clearly. I'm sure this has to do with the fact that your face is beat to hell. I look down at the bandage on your foot. Blood has begun to seep through, and it needs to be tended to. I need you to move; I need you to get up. It appears you won't be able to stand, even though I desperately need you to. But it takes a considerable amount of effort for you to remain sitting in the upright position, so standing hardly seems likely.

"Order him off," he tells me, and it takes me a second to understand what he means. "Your dog," he adds. "Shut him up."

"He's a dog," I shrug. "He barks."

"That's no dog. That's a well-oiled machine."

I think about what he's just said, and it's too bad I let Roscoe out. He didn't want to go—I had to force him—a decision I now regret. Now, he's going crazy in the backyard, and I'm more afraid of him waking the kids than I am of one of the neighbors coming 'round. I walk over to the back door, and I consider my proximity to the nearest gun. Our guest follows, unfortunately, and it'd be taking a risk, making a move now.

"Don't open it," he says, motioning toward the door. "I don't want to have to shoot your dog."

I knock on the door and give the sign calling Roscoe off. He stops barking, but he doesn't settle. "Back to the kitchen," he says, and I don't immediately go, which turns out to be a mistake when he picks up a picture of the kids and holds it up to eye level. "Nice family," he quips, and I start for the kitchen. He follows.

"He's in bad shape…" he says looking down at you.

I press my lips together, and I don't disagree, but there isn't anything to say, so I say nothing.

I want to be mad at you for getting yourself in this situation, and I won't lie, there's a part of me that is. But the other part wants to take this slow—let it work itself out. After all, there is light at the end of the tunnel, the chance that we can all get what we want. Still, there's a tug-o-war going on inside of me. I don't want to give her up, and I sure as hell don't want to let him win, not after what he's done to you. I consider the disaster this is, a man holding us at gunpoint, our children upstairs in bed. It's not ideal, to put it mildly. But she always did say she wanted to see him one last time so maybe there's a silver lining here somewhere. It would be nice if we could all get what we want, but even I'm not that optimistic a person.

I turn my attention toward him. "I assume you're here about Cheryl," I say, and then I nod at the condition you're in. I don't know how much you've told him, but I'm guessing everything, seeing that he showed up here and drug you along with him.

"So he did tell you about her then," he replies, and he folds his lips, as though my knowing is disappointing. "I figured as much."

I cock my head and glance at you. I don't understand what he means. You immediately look away, which tells me everything I need to know. You haven't told him anything.

He steadies his gun, aims it directly at your forehead. "No," he tells me. "This isn't just about her," he sighs. "It's about the truth."

"The truth," I repeat, and then I cross my arms. "Then what?" I ask, and I uncross them, flinging my hands in the air. It's dramatic, that's what you're thinking, but this whole fucking ordeal is dramatic. He doesn't say anything. I don't think he was expecting my reaction. I shake my head. "After the truth—what happens then? You kill him— you kill me— but where does that leave you?"

"I'll be fine," he says, eying my hand on the kettle. It's dangerous for him to let me around fire, around boiling water specifically, but then he doesn't know what I'm capable of. That much is clear.

"Why don't you tell him, Kate," you say and your words

are slow to come and garbled. "Tell him what he wants to hear...Tell him the truth."

I consider making good on your advice, telling him that she's alive, that she's upstairs, letting him in on his happily ever after. I know you're trying to dissuade me from pouring boiling water on the guy. I know that's why you say what you say. Otherwise you would've told him yourself. You can't stand to see me come out the hero here. But someone has to save this ship, which is why something, a tiny feeling in the pit of my stomach, stops me. First things first— I don't like the way he's treated you. This was my fault—I'm the one who took her; you didn't deserve the blame. I take a deep breath, pour the steaming water into my mug, and drop a tea bag in. I consider my next move but first I remove another mug from the cabinet and make you a cup. Then I raise my brow in his direction. It's a question he answers by telling me he doesn't like tea. "Leave his," he says, and I don't like his tone. I don't like that he thinks he can tell me what to do in my own home. More so, I don't know why she thinks he's so great—I'm liking him less and less by the minute.

I watch as he drags a kitchen chair over to you and sits down. It irritates me. He has no concern for noise, and he's violating my space. But what it also tells me is that he hasn't considered that our children are upstairs.

"Hmmm," I murmur, and I position myself correctly. "About the book," I say. "She knew if I returned it to you, it would lead you here eventually, didn't she?"

"It appears that way," he says, raising his brow. "She was a smart woman."

"She was," I reply. "But I still don't get it... what is it you want from us?" I ask. I raise my shoulders and let them fall. "Why'd you come?"

"Like I said—I want answers. I want the truth. I want her

to have a proper burial…" he tells me and then looks away, down at you. "But most of all— I want revenge."

"And if she were alive? What then?"

He scoffs. "She's not alive," he tells me, and he shakes his head at the stupidity of such a suggestion. "She wouldn't— she couldn't— have stayed away. Not this long."

"Unless someone was seeing to it that she did."

"Even then. Not without an email—not without a phone call… you don't understand a love like ours. We didn't go around second-guessing whether or not to stay or go. Not like you."

I smile. "I didn't think you did," I say. I blow on my tea, take a sip, and then take the cup over to you. He follows me with his gun, watching closely as I place the cup to your lips. You sip slowly, but you don't drink much. It's okay because what you really need is water. I figured the heat would help your throat. I was wrong. You cough, and you nearly choke. He gets antsy and eventually I move away.

"I don't know what you plan to do here," I say to him, and then I pause, because I'm annoyed. I want to play this care- fully. He isn't going to get away with what he's done and neither is she. She brought this on, and he finished it by coming here. All along she wanted me to make a choice, you or her, and I know you felt the same way. Well, I've made my choice, and it's you. It's always been you. "But whatever it is —" I say to him. "Maybe we outta get on with it."

"I see," he answers, folding his lips. "So, I take it you're not going to tell me what happened to her."

"What's the point? You've already made up your mind. You want revenge."

"In that case—" he starts. He pauses and shakes his head. He does so slowly, as though all along he was afraid that's what I'd say. Afraid that he might actually have to make a move. "Well, in that case," he says looking at you. "The plan goes like this—first, I shoot you in front of your husband. He's next."

I exhale.

He repositions the gun and stands. He wants me to see that he's serious. He stops abruptly and backhands you. He's a controlled man, like you, not quick to anger, not quick to let his next move show. He either doesn't know what he plans to do next, or he isn't ready to do it. I decide to offer up more of the same. I grip the kettle and start to lift it from the stove.

You start to make a move, which means I'm going to need my hands to be free, and so I set it back down. It would be difficult given where he's standing to douse him anyway, not without hitting you.

I clear my throat and meet his gaze. "That— or I could just give you the answers you came for. You never know. You might find yourself pleasantly surprised."

He faces me and considers what I've said. He's trying to figure out what it might mean and whether he can take whatever it is I have to say. I can see he clearly wants to believe in a happy ending but he won't let himself go there. I face the stairwell, he faces me. We're in a silent standoff, he wants to ask for more but it seems he can't make himself. I was hoping you'd help me out here but you won't. You can't. You're sitting back against the kitchen counter, hunched over, head hanging. I'm not even sure you're still conscious at this point, not after that blow.

He sees me eyeing you. "He's pretty out of it...could be a concussion—" he shrugs. "Or it could be a brain bleed. Heaven knows he's taken enough hits. In any case—not much he can do to help you now."

He aims the gun at my chest, and I hate the way he reads me. He's like you in that way, and a tiny part of me does suddenly see why he appeals to her. "So let's have it."

"Cher—is—" I start to say but I stutter when I see Brady moving from the corner of my eye. However my death will come, I can guarantee one thing, it won't be in front of my child. I grip the teapot, lifting it fully. He orders me to put it down. When I look past him, over his shoulder, I see Brady is descending the stairs, step by quiet step. Also, it's worse than I first thought. He's holding your revolver. As he lifts it and takes aim, I say a silent prayer. I praise Rudy for going behind my back, for teaching him to shoot, and I hope with everything in me that the target practice pays off.

~

OUR VISITOR TAKES A BULLET TO THE LOWER ABDOMEN. He doesn't see it coming, in part thanks to the silencer. Brady puts one more in his kneecap before I manage to yell. That gets his attention. He places the gun on the floor at his feet. He's sensitive to raised voices. I run to him, lean down slowly, and pick the gun up. "Go to Liv's room and lock the door," I say hugging him tight. He doesn't like to be touched, but he doesn't move away. He doesn't squeeze back, and he isn't scared like most six year olds would be. He's emotionless. I run my fingers through his hair and pull back, looking him in the eye. "You did a good job Brady—"

He searches my face, his eyes large and irrevocably calm. He shakes his head, and pulls away and reaches for the gun. "No," I tell him.

He furrows his little brow, and tilts his head to the side. "But he's not dead. Grandpa says I have to make them dead."

I close my eyes, just for a split-second and I rub at the back of my neck. I move the gun away, out of his reach. "It's ok," I promise and we both look over at the man on the floor. He's moaning, bleeding out quickly. Stomach wounds tend to do that. He tries to scoot himself toward the door, and all I can think about is the giant mess he's making—nothing that a little bleach and water won't take care of, and now I understand why you wouldn't let me have the tile I originally wanted. Blood would be a nightmare to get out of grout. All of a sudden, I'm incredibly grateful for your forethought. He moves painstakingly slowly, there's not much use. But I get a better hold on the gun just in case. Also, I think it's time that he and Roscoe became acquainted. I fold my lips and then I walk over and retrieve his weapon. It's now halfway across the room where Brady kicked it. I look down at him, and then I open the door. Roscoe bolts in and takes a defensive position. He sniffs your face and then immediately goes to Brady's side.

"Don't worry Coco," Brady says. That's what the kids call him. Olivia never could quite say Roscoe. "It's okay."

I lean down and offer Roscoe a hand signal to let him know what he needs to do. "Do as I said, Brady. Go up to Olivia's room. Stay there until I come for you."

"Is Daddy okay?" he asks, looking at you. You've fallen over onto your side, and it's apparent you're now fully unconscious.

I check your pulse. I don't want to do it in front of him but I can't make myself wait. Finally, I breathe a sigh of relief, feeling the blood as it moves through your veins. "He will be," I say. "Now go—"

He doesn't move, not at first. He just stands there, staring at me for a minute, and then when he's ready, he turns and goes. I watch as he reluctantly climbs the stairs. Roscoe stays put. When he vanishes from my line of sight I kneel down and I study the man's face. "This is going to be impossible to clean up," I tell him. His eyes are closed, and he doesn't answer. "It's too bad," I continue. "Because your girlfriend is upstairs."

He opens his eyes slowly then, and I'm not sure what it is I see in them. Confusion, maybe. Fear, for sure.

"Hang tight," I say, patting his shoulder and I stand and take a step backward. Then I put a bullet in his other kneecap. Better to be safe than sorry. Roscoe is good, but sometimes the easy way is better. He moans loudly, writhes from side to side, and eventually lays his head back on our proper flooring. That's what you called it, proper flooring. I can see it clearly now, the day we fought over it, the day you picked it out, and said you weren't budging. I smile remembering.

I take a few steps over to you. "Jude," I call, slapping your cheek. You inhale and then exhale, quietly, but you don't wake up. Still, it tells me you can hear me. It's a good sign. Brady meanders back down the stairs with a first aid kit. "I can fix him," he says, looking at me, and my heart breaks. He's so matter of fact. Almost like he's not seeing what's in front of him at all. He's simply going through the motions, and that scares me the most. "Brady," I say, contemplating how to rectify the situation. "Help me get Daddy into the living room…"

He sets the kit down. I tell him to take your hands and I take your feet and slowly, ever so slowly, we slide your limp body across the floor. When we make it to the living room, he props a couch cushion under your head and plops down beside you. I stand there panting, trying to catch my breath. You open your eyes just barely, and you smile slightly.

I place my hands on my hips and stand upright. I lighten my tone. I make it fake-happy, chipper. "You see, Buddy," I say to him. "Daddy is going to be fine. He just needs to rest."

"Ice," he tells me. "He needs ice."

"And ice, yes."

"And a band-aid."

"That too," I say.

He nods, and I can see the wheels turning behind his eyes. He stands. I can't let him go back in that kitchen.

"Listen—" I tell him. "I'm going to let you help me take care of Daddy—but first I need to take care of other things. That means I need you to go to your sister's room, lock the door, and stay with her. Can you do that for me?"

He studies my face, my whole face, he takes it all in, processing it in the only way he can. Eventually, he nods his head up and down.

"It's your job to protect her," I add and I can see that something clicks for him.

"I will protect Livy," he promises and I lean in and kiss the top of his head. Tears fill my eyes because he isn't a talker. He doesn't communicate, not much, but it's clear now, he gets it. It's clear he gets it all.

~

"COME WITH ME," I DEMAND, PULLING HER OUT OF BED. Obviously she's confused, which is why she stalls. These aren't normal visiting hours—that, and she never leaves this room. I point the gun at her. "I have something to show you," I say. "I think you'll be happy to see what it is."

She stands and pats her head. She's still disoriented from being woken abruptly and it shows. "Where are we—"

"No talking," I say, cutting her off. "Just wait and see."

We take the side stairs down to the kitchen, the same ones Brady took. "Kate," she says, pausing, and I ram the gun into her back. It's a warning. She takes it for what it is, and she doesn't say anything else. She shuts her mouth, and she keeps going forward. "Please—just get it over with," she tells me, pausing again, teetering on one of the steps. I nudge her onward.

When we reach the bottom of the stairs, she stops dead in her tracks. Her hands fly to her mouth. "Oh my God!"

He looks up at the sound of her voice. "Cheryl?"

In an instant, she rushes to his side and hits her knees. I watch as she presses her hand to his stomach. When she pulls it away, it's covered in blood. She stares at it, eyes widened, and quickly places her hand back over the wound. She looks at me, and then around the room, in search of something. When she doesn't find anything worthwhile, she glances back at me, pleading with her eyes. She wants me to fix what she broke. But you can't fix trust. Betrayal is a funny beast that way.

"You're alive," he says.

"Look at you," she tells him, eyeing him from head to toe.

I move a chair and sit down. "The book," I say.

She turns her attention to me. I look over at Roscoe, lying at your side.

"It was all a ploy, wasn't it? All these months... you've been leading up to this. You made me promise I'd go see him, made me promise I'd return it. You said it would bring closure, and for what?" I demand, and I shake my head from side to side. "To save your ass—that's for what."

"Kate..."

"You knew he would come for us— you knew it all along — and you played me," I say, opening the chamber, checking the number of bullets. I know you, you're always prepared, so I shouldn't worry, but I do. It's unwarranted, you have me covered, and I love you for the way you see things in advance. I should have seen this coming. But I didn't. Maybe you didn't either. But you made sure the gun was fully loaded, and you insured that we had proper flooring, and it's the little things that end up meaning the most.

She doesn't respond to me. She doesn't try to defend

herself. She doesn't care what I think. She simply touches his face.

I take another sip of my tea, but it's gone cold. "You should see what he did to Jude…"

"I'm sorry—" she tells me then. "I just needed to see him one last time. I needed to know there was a chance. Surely, you can understand—"

"It doesn't matter what I understand—" I say. "It matters that you almost got me killed. We were supposed to be friends."

"We are friends, Kate. We are."

"I don't think so."

She shifts and then she pushes herself up to a standing position. She's wearing those pajamas I bought her way back when. Back when there was still hope. Back when I thought she would help us. When I thought she was good.

She comes toward me, her hand outstretched. "We can work this out Kate, I know we can."

I shake my head. "There are a few things you should know about me Cheryl…you betrayed me. That's not something I take lightly. Your selfishness is the reason you're going to die in the end. It's the reason he's going to die," I say, pointing to her lover. "That makes you a murderer, too."

"Kate—"

"No—" I say, cutting her off. "You made me out to be a fool. My husband has been beaten, and my child has just shot a man. Twice. I don't think there's any coming back from that," I say, and then I sigh. "In fact, I'll be lucky if either of them forgive me for this."

"They will. Jude loves you. We all make mistakes…"

"Yes," I tell her. "And mine was not killing you in the first place."

"Kate," she pleads, holding her hands out. They're big

hands. That's what I see in the end. When she takes another step forward, I pull the trigger. No need to drag this out.

He cries out as she goes down. She lands next to him with a thud. I lean down and press the gun to his chest. "I'd shoot you in the head," I say. "But it's messier that way."

"Please," he cries.

"I really don't like it when people beg," I tell him. "What I also don't like is when I do the right thing, and it backfires on me. That book was a peace offering. And this—" I tell him, gesturing around the kitchen, "is not what I call peace."

"I—" he starts to say, but I cut him off.

"You see— that's how I know what needs to be done. Cheryl was my friend," I say, rolling my eyes. "Or so I thought. That is, until you showed up and ruined everything. We had a good system going here." I look around the kitchen. "Not anymore," I add, shaking my head, looking down at her cold, dead eyes. "You know…I'll have to take care of this, and it won't be easy. I'll have to clean all of this up—and who is going to help? Not you. You can't even stand up. My husband can't help—look at him. Look what you've done."

"I'm sorry," he begs.

"Me too—sorry that I have to correct this mess— sorry that I'll have to pretend it never happened. And I have you to thank for that."

"But it did happen."

"You should have left well enough alone," I whisper, eyeing the bodies on the floor. "We were happy here. But not you. You and your little affair, well— it wreaked havoc on our lives. If it weren't for you, we never would have met Cheryl. And none of this would have happened."

"I'm sorry," he pleads again.

"You had to have her though. Didn't you? So you had her get my husband involved. You wanted her all for yourself—

you wanted her husband gone, out of the picture— and look what it's cost us."

"What has it cost you, really?" he asks, closing his eyes again. I take it for what it is—a clue that he's on his way out. Also, an admission of guilt. "Yes," he says, surprising me. "I did tell her to hire him. But that's where it ended. I didn't want all of this. I had no idea she was alive. If I had—I would have gone about it another way, I swear to you…" he cracks then, breaks down. "I swear—I thought her husband killed her. I just thought Jude had answers that's all…I didn't know…"

"What has it cost me?" I sneer. "Let me tell you what it cost. My pride, for starters. And Jude—well, he's hurt. Do you think I like seeing my husband in this condition? No— I don't. Also, I just shot the person I thought was my one and only friend. That's what it cost me. All because you couldn't keep your dick in your pants."

"She wasn't your friend."

"You know—it's funny," I tell him and a small laugh manages to escape. "That's the only thing you've said tonight that makes any sense. You're right about that. She wasn't my friend. And that's why she's dead."

"Please—" he utters. I don't let him finish. I never did care for beggars. I press the gun to his beating heart, and I fire.

∾

CHAPTER THIRTEEN

JUDE

"I really hate this," you say as you change my dressing. You don't do it softly, and you're not careful. You're punishing me.

I wince. "It doesn't look like you hate it."

"I do, Jude," you tell me, pausing what you're doing, which is the worst thing you could do, because the longer it takes, the more it hurts. "I really, really do—hate it."

After you're finished cleaning me up, you bring me my lunch. It's one of those microwave meals, and it's terrible. I eat it anyway, because I need my strength. That, and I won't let you win. I have to heal; I have to get out of here. It's cold and that helps with motivation. I ask for another blanket but it never comes. "Now, you know what I meant before," you say, and even though neither of us brings up *before*, we both know what you mean by it.

I shake at my tether. It's twisted. I don't really see the point of it, we both know it's all for show. I doubt I would get far, not in this condition. You're reading, and you pay me no attention. I shake harder and eventually you look over. I nod at it and slowly your gaze follows. "I don't know why I have to have this thing," I tell you. "It's not like I'm going anywhere."

You jut out your bottom lip and then you move to help me out. "You always say I'm not good at safety measures. I'm proving you wrong."

I exhale and watch you sit back down. You return your attention to the book in your hands. *Misery*. How fitting.

"It's just, you need to forgive me, that's all," you say, but you don't look up. When I don't respond, you take my covers away.

"Forgiveness is hard," I reply, "when you keep me locked up in here. It gives me a lot of time to think…"

"It's for your own good," you tell me. "With your foot like that, and your face looking like it went through a meat grinder, I can't exactly let you out into the world. What would the neighbors think?"

"Who cares what the neighbors think?"

You look up and your eyes are challenging. "I do."

YOU WERE KIND ENOUGH TO HAVE A DOCTOR COME AND PATCH me up, I'll give you that. Although, I don't remember much of it. I do remember him and another quack carrying me up those stairs, though. I remember the way my ribs screamed; I remember the pain, how every step felt a little closer to death. I remember that, inch by horrific inch, it felt like I was climbing the stairway to hell.

I remember waking up, tethered to this bed, the same as she was. It's easy to see what your plan is here. You're trying to teach me a lesson; you think I'm another one of your pets. "You're a lucky man," the doctor told me on our way up those stairs, and I don't know what you paid that guy to keep this kind of thing quiet but it's amazing how people surprise me.

For the right price and a little finesse, you can buy anything you want. Apparently.

"He shot himself in the foot," you joked, and everyone had a good laugh. Everyone but me.

"He messed with the wrong woman," another of the guys said, and that much was accurate.

"What are you thinking about?" you ask, interrupting my thoughts.

I fold my lips. "Nothing."

You check the time on your phone, stand and stretch. "The kids will be home soon," you say, and I know it's time for you to go. I hate that it bothers me to see you walk out that door, but it does. "I'll send them in," you promise.

You do at least let them visit. Olivia says I have to stay here in case the bad guys come looking again, and that seems to make sense to them. I would correct your little story, but I'm not sure I can break their hearts by telling them the truth.

You think this is funny, that it is some sort of game, and I don't know how I'll ever pay you back for this kind of misery, but I will. You can't keep me here forever.

≈

"I was hungry, Kate. You need to be better about bringing my meals on time," I tell you, because I know your lag time was about more than your little victory meeting. I know you're punishing me.

"I'm sorry," you say. "I was sick. I ate something bad, and I was up all night…"

I roll my eyes. "Sorry to hear that. I ate nothing."

"Well, I'm sorry about it, too. I don't think I'll ever be able to eat quiche again."

"I don't like it when you stay away so long," I say, and I

hate how much I mean it. It's lonely in this room, with nothing but an expanse of hours stretched out in front of you. It's like a road to nowhere, and I want to stay strong. I want to hate you. I want to stay angry—but every day forgiveness is looking better and better.

"I have a lot on my plate," you tell me. "You can't always come first. Plus, I had to take care of things with the attorney," you say, dusting your hands together.

"How'd that go?" I ask and I hold my breath.

"Very well. I agreed to drop the lawsuit against the school and in turn they've agreed to recant their story about the whole arson misunderstanding. They've agreed to drop it all," you say, clapping your hands.

"It must feel good to get your way," I reply. "But do you really think a lawsuit was the way to go? Drawing attention to us and all?"

"I wasn't trying to draw attention to us. They kicked our kid out of school—refused to admit that he was being bullied —not just emotionally—but physically. You saw his face. You heard what those boys did. Then he set the school on fire and well—you'll have to forgive me. I was trying to keep our son from having a rap sheet at the tender age of six."

"Maybe—" I counter. "But in the process, you became exactly the kind of sue-happy person we've always hated. Lest you forget that's why we do what we do with the killing —we leave the system out of it," I say, and I instantly regret it. I shouldn't put ideas in your head. Not the way your last pet did.

You cock your head, and squint your eyes. "Whatever. And—I haven't gotten my way. Don't forget, while you're laid up in here whining about your foot "healing," I had to find them a new school. Which I hated to do—not only because it was a pain in the ass—but also because it feels like giving in. Also, it's embarrassing," you add. You shrug, like it's nothing, an afterthought, "They seem to like it, though."

"How much is this one costing us?"

You shift your gaze. "That's nothing you need to worry about. Not in your condition…"

"We need to talk about the school—about the money."

"I told you. It's nothing you need to concern yourself with."

"With me not working, and the attorney's fees, it is."

"I told you. 'Boobs' from the grocery store helped us out."

"What's your definition of 'helped'?"

"She was the attorney who made this all go away…"

"Vanessa? I thought you hated her," I say, and I don't remember you telling me you were using her.

"I do. But big boobs and favors take you far in life. Let's just say, I called one in."

"What is that supposed to mean?"

Your eyes light up and you smile. "Well, since you're sitting down…"

∽

"SAY THAT AGAIN."

"Vanessa. Our neighbor," you say, and you take your time, drawing it out. "You know—the one we ran into at the grocery store. The one we've had in our home," you add, but you talk too slowly. "Turns out her husband has a thing for meeting women online…"

"And why should I care about what her husband does?"

"Those girls… The ones she mentioned that day on aisle six?" You're talking faster now. "Well, let's just say, she knew more than she let on. A lot more…"

I do a double-take. "What the fuck?"

"That's what I said."

"Scott? The one who offered to help with our plumbing… you're telling me, he's responsible for killing multiple women? No way," I say. "That guy can barely string two sentences together."

"Not Scott—Vanessa."

"She killed them?"

You nod. "Jealousy…rage…I guess they do things to people."

My eyes widen. I hadn't seen that one coming. But you're speaking too passionately to be lying. "I guess so."

"But a favor is a favor," you say. Then you shrug. "And I needed one."

I tilt my head and study your face. You're not one to joke about things like this, but seriously? "You're not the least bit concerned that she knows you know?"

You shake your head. "I didn't tell her I know, silly—I'm not stupid."

"Neither is she, apparently."

You wave me off. "Anyway, we're good. I think we have an understanding between us."

I fold my arms and study you. "You think?"

"Blackmail is a beautiful thing, my love."

"It's a dangerous thing."

You pat my head, and you stand to go. "Tell you what—I'll come back when you're in a better mood."

It's a lie. You wouldn't know about my mood because you don't come back for two days. But at least I don't have to worry so much about retribution for you keeping me tied up, in this room. Looks like you've got a pretty good handle on that yourself. Typical, Kate. Sticking your nose where it doesn't belong. Doing that will get you killed. I know, the last time you tried these antics I ended up here. Let's hope for both our sakes, things turn out better this time.

~

"I NEED TO GET BACK TO WORK," I TELL YOU ONE MORNING over coffee.

"What for? We have more than enough in savings…"

I study you, something is different. You're sitting up straighter than normal, and I can see there's something you're not telling me. "You're up to your old antics, aren't you?"

"No…" you lie. "I'm too busy dealing with you," you tell me, and you walk over and adjust the pillow behind my head. "You're a very demanding patient, you know."

I grab ahold of your wrist. "That could be handled," I say, looking into your eyes. "It's not exactly like I want to be your patient, Kate."

You look away toward the tether. "Why don't you just fight your way out?"

I wait for you to look up at me. You don't. "I'll never understand why she didn't fight more. I don't get why she never tried…"

"I don't know…" I say. "Me? I have three broken ribs and a hole in my foot. How far do you really think I'm going to get? Plus… I'm not scared of you. I'll heal in time. As for her, I think she wanted to be here, a part of her did. I think she wanted to see if he'd come."

You meet my eyes then. "You think?"

"I don't think much of her, no."

"You're right—" you exclaim. I heard the surprise in your tone, and it catches me off guard. "I think she knew her husband was going to kill her…. I think he found out about the affair, and that was that. She came to you…"

"Probably," I say, and you let it go. "Whatever it was, it seems she had a plan…"

I let your wrist go. You know I don't like talking about her.

You take two steps back to your chair and you slump down into it. "So, what's *your* plan?"

"Me—" I ask motioning toward my chest. "Oh, I plan to run as far as I can get."

You cock one eyebrow. I don't think you believe me. "And the kids?"

"We'll share custody."

You laugh, and it's the angry kind. "That's not going to work."

"Why not? Couples do it every day."

"I don't," you tell me, and your voice drops. "Not every day—not on *any* day."

I look away. "We don't have to discuss this now," I say. We both know where things stand. There's no sense in driving the point home. I close my eyes. "It will all work out…"

You roll your eyes, but I see the hurt in them. "If you say so."

I can see now this wasn't the way you expected this to go. But this latest incident—this latest series of bad decisions you made— they're a short list in the grand scheme of all you've done. "It's not that I don't love you Kate. It's just that I can't keep doing this."

I watch you rub at your jaw. "You plan on killing me… you're not going to admit it, of course, but I see it in your eyes. Plus, I sort of have the upper hand right now…"

"No," I tell you, but even you can see that I'm lying. "I don't plan to kill you."

"What are you waiting for?" you ask. But as the words escape your lips, I see that recognition takes over. Your eyes narrow. "You're making me take care of you—nurse you back to health—you're using me—until you don't need me. That's what you're waiting for…I'm disposable." You let out a small laugh. "That's funny, you know. Cheryl warned me this would happen."

I cock my head. Two can play the hurting game, Kate. You'll see. "If you say so."

～

YOU STAY AWAY FOR TWO DAYS. I NEED MY PAIN MEDS, AND food would be nice, but you don't care. I have a lot of time on my hands, lots of time to think. And you know what I've been thinking about…I've been wondering if you think it's odd that we so freely and so frequently discuss killing one another. Something tells me that's not the norm in the average marriage. Not that I've ever aspired to be average. But, that said, you'll be happy to know that I've given it some thought, and I don't want you dead after all. I want to come to an agreement—an understanding. It's kind of hard to do that if you won't show your face.

When you do finally come in, you look like hell.

"What's wrong?" I ask, trying to sit up. I can't. It hurts too much. "Is it the kids?"

You swallow hard, and my stomach flip-flops. It could be the hunger or it could be the look in your eyes, maybe both. "I think it's time to settle this," you say.

I suck in my bottom lip.

"This animosity between us. It's not healthy."

I don't say anything. I know it's best to let you talk.

You place a tray down on my lap. It's actual food, not one of those microwave meals you've been punishing me with. "I saw your father today…" you tell me nonchalantly. "He didn't ask about you."

"That's not surprising," I say, and I wish I hadn't had that fight with him because certainly he'd be looking for me now, and you'd be forced to give up this whole charade. It's only been a little over a week but I don't know how long this can go on. Unless we're considering how long you kept your last captive locked away, and well, I realize, in that case, it could be awhile.

I take a bite of my sandwich, and I've never tasted anything so good. I chew slowly, and then I swallow. It could be poison, for all I care. My stomach seizes, I swallow. "What needs settling anyway?"

"Remember when you killed your ex-girlfriend, and in turn led that guy here? You know—the one who beat me nearly to death and killed our unborn baby in the process?"

"Kate."

"No!" you say, raising your voice. "Answer me. Do you— or do you not— remember?"

"I'm not dignifying such a ridiculous, cruel question with an answer."

"Good," you nod. "You remember. Because what I did isn't much different. And if I'm going to let you out of here, then I'm going to need to know that you forgive me."

"You nearly got me killed. You nearly got our *entire family* killed."

"So did you," you say, and you have a point, even if I hate to admit it. Also, it's not the same.

I take the banana from the tray and peel it. Then I look up at you. "What are you suggesting?"

"I'm suggesting that we put this whole thing behind us. Move on with our lives—get happy again."

"Happiness comes second to safety. And you've proven time and time again—you're not good at it."

"I could bring in another therapist if you think that would help."

"Ha. Ha."

"What?" you say, gesturing around the small space. "The two of you could be roommates."

"I'm not having this conversation." I know you're joking. But still. I'm not in the mood for your games.

"Fine," you reply. "But, just so you know, it would have to be a guy… given the bathroom sharing thing…"

I exhale and let it out sharply. "Stop."

"Where's your sense of humor anyway?

"Trapped in this room, like the rest of me."

You smile and you rub your hand up my thigh. I catch your wrist. You look up at me and it kills any and all resolve I might have had. "Do you think you're healed enough to have sex?"

I change the subject. Mostly, because I know the answer is no. My ribs can't take it. "How about you tell me what you did with the bodies before I make that call."

You jut out your bottom lip and pout like the child you are. "Guess you're not bored enough yet."

I shrug, and it hurts like a motherfucker. It sucks when I forget about the pain. "Tell me Kate…"

"I did."

"No—you didn't? Not really."

You take a deep breath in, and you let it out all at once. "I took them out to the barn. Burned them. Buried the bones."

"Separately."

You furrow your brow. "Of course, separately."

"Good God—I hope you're telling the truth."

You offer a weak smile. "Why wouldn't I be?"

I gulp the rest of my sandwich down, and I refuse to dignify that question with an answer.

WHEN YOU COME IN THE NEXT DAY, YOU HAND ME SOMETHING. I don't immediately look at it, I'm too busy eyeing the take-out you've brought. Finally, some real food.

"Olivia made you a get well card."

I nod and I read in your expression that something is off. "What is it now?"

You sit down, prop your feet up on me. "Look at the card."

I'm too busy looking at the food. Peas, carrots...I lift the tray closer to my face, and it hurts, but I inhale slowly. "Is that lamb?"

"Yes."

"Since when have we eaten lamb?"

You fold your arms. "Open the card."

I do as you ask, and a slip of paper falls into my lap. I pick it up, glance at it, and then look over at you.

"I'm pregnant."

I look back at the ultrasound photo, and I shake my head. "What? How?"

You narrow your eyes. "Seriously?"

I don't say anything for a long while. I just stare at the photo. "I thought we were done."

"In every sense of the word, apparently." You look away and then back at me. Anger seeps through the air and catches like wildfire. "We could always give it to Josie."

I study my hands. "You're not serious."

"Of course, I'm not serious," you say. "I can raise three kids on my own—it's no biggie."

"That's the thing," I reply. I look down at the ultrasound photo and then over at you. "I don't want you to."

You smile, but I'm not sure you really mean it. "Eat," you say and I scarf down your news, and then the lamb, baby carrots, and peas. It's not what I would've chosen, but it seems to make perfect sense.

~

A FEW DAYS LATER YOU COME IN AND YOU'RE A DIFFERENT

Kate. You're the upswing Kate. On top of the world Kate. "We're moving," you say excitedly. I expected something wild and crazy. But not this.

"We're what?"

You sit down next to me. The movement hurts. "I found a house."

I wait for you to say more but you don't. "Why would we move?"

You shrug and you take away my dishes, and then stand to take a look at my bandage. I wince as you unwrap it. "We're having another kid…this place isn't big enough…"

"It's plenty big." I tell you. "People do with a lot less."

"I want a fresh start," you say, and now you're starting to make sense. Not much. But some.

"It's in Asheville," you mention. You stop what you're doing, reach into your pocket and hand me a photo of the listing. "I just need your signature."

"Why North Carolina?"

"Because," you said. "I told you. I want a change… I want seasons."

"You didn't say change. You said a fresh start."

"Same difference."

I look at the listing and I don't get it. You love it here. I look up at you. "What do you want me to say?"

"I want you to say you like it."

I glance back at the photo. "It's okay, I guess."

"Good," you clap. "I'm glad you like it…because I signed for you."

"This is about the blackmail thing, isn't it?"

You raise your shoulders and let them drop slowly. Then you throw up your hands. You don't like it when I see right through you. "You're the one who said it was dangerous. I just thought it would be nice to put a little distance between us and danger."

"Sounds about right…"

"Safety measures, darling," you tell me with a smile. "Otherwise, I'd have to kill them." You nod in my direction. "You're in no shape to do it," you say. "And I'm pregnant…"

～

I CONTINUE TO HEAL, AND THE CLOSER WE GET TO MOVING day, the better I start to feel. You take the kids out of school. It's too risky. Shortly thereafter you let me out of that room. It helps that my ribs were healed enough to allow me to make it down the stairs. That's not to say the coming down part was much fun. It wasn't. But the kids were driving you crazy. Also, morning sickness, and blackmail, make your decision easy. Seems to me a little like karma at work. But you need me; you need help.

One morning, you're taping up boxes, and Josie stops by to offer her assistance. She's the only one we've told we're leaving, and I didn't even want to tell her, but it's a quick move, and with me in the condition I'm in, and the fact that you're throwing up every 2.5 seconds, we had no choice but to let Josie do what she does best.

"A new job," she says looking at me but speaking to you. "I just don't know how a new job could take you away. You guys love it here."

She's seriously distraught, and I would guess contemplating a move herself.

"The offer was right," you say, and you look over at me.

"Aren't you going to miss this place?" she asks. "Just think of all the memories you made here…"

Your eyes glaze over, and I can see that your mind is going there.

Mine does too. I think back to the first time I brought you here. I think about how you broke the baby news to me then. I think about the days that turned into months, the months that turned into years. I think about birthday parties, first steps, and the lines on the mudroom wall marking our children's growth. I think of the good times and the bad, and all the times in between.

"A lot of memories," you say to Josie. But you study my face. You know what I'm thinking.

"How about this?" she asks, holding up a glass vase. She's already moved on.

"That stays," you tell her.

We're not taking much. Just the items that mean something. That makes it easy. I'm watching you as she holds up another item, and you shake your head. It's all happening so fast and simultaneously, it seems like slow motion. You stand and stretch. You arch your back, and I can see your belly is rounder already. You've never looked more beautiful. I want to be angry with myself just a little for thinking as much; I want to be mad at myself for loving you, but in the end, I'm only human. Plus, of all the people on this planet, you seem like one who could use love the most. It wasn't supposed to be this way, I wasn't supposed to stick around. I don't consider myself a forgiving person. But there's a lot to consider, other than just what I want, and so here I am, looking at you, looking forward to a fresh start, looking forward to new memories.

∼

"YOU'RE GOING TO MAKE SO MANY MEMORIES," MY FATHER SAID to me. We're standing on the tarmac, the way you used to be able to do, before everyone's freedoms were taken, before flying commercial became the nightmare it is today. I'm not sure why he said that; he isn't a sentimental guy. It's likely he couldn't think of anything else to say. That, and if I had to guess, I'm sure he felt bad sending me away. My mother didn't come to the airport to see me off. She was too sick. I knew she didn't think it was a good idea, my father sending me to Sri Lanka, no matter how much she liked Bob. She needed me there. I knew it, and she knew it, and in a sense, even my father knew it. That was half of the reason I think he made me go. I heard them fighting about it late at night for weeks prior to my departure date.

My mother, who hated losing, decided to soothe her anger by going on a three-day bender right before I was set to leave. I barely saw her those last few days. I stood at the foot of her bed and told her goodbye. If she could lift her head, she didn't. She stared at the ceiling. "I'm sick because you're leaving, Jude. Just sick."

"I can see that," I told her.

"I'm sorry— I can't go to the airport to see you off."

"It's fine."

"You're going to like it there. I have a feeling."

"I like it here," I said, and I tried to make it sound as sincere as I meant it, hoping at last they'd change their mind, and let me stay.

"You think that now," she told me, and her eyes shifted slightly but she didn't look my way. "In time though, you'll come to see how good it can be to have a fresh start."

~

KNOWING WE'RE LEAVING THIS TOWN, I REALIZE THERE'S ONLY one thing left to do. I have to tell my father goodbye. He doesn't know we're moving. He and I haven't spoken since the day he tried to talk me into killing you.

I don't go to his house; I go to the one place I know I'll find him this time of day. I drive to the marina. It's sunny out, but still chilly, and I haven't brought a jacket. I walk with a limp, I still have bruising here and there, and I still lean to one side. Going to see my father in this condition is the last thing I wanted to do, because in a way it's a concession, proof to him that he was right all along. It's his confirmation that I can't handle you, that I can't manage my own life, that I'm not in control of my affairs. I considered this a lot before setting out on this drive, but in the end, I realize, it's now or never, and this is too important to let a few bruises get in the way.

When I arrive, he's prepping the boat. He's close to backing out of his slip, just as I knew he would be. I hop on board, slowly and painfully, with donuts in hand, just like always. He looks up, but he doesn't stop what he's doing.

"I brought donuts," I say, although that much is obvious. I'm holding them. He glances down at the bag.

I sit down and make myself comfortable. "You know I don't fish with company."

"Not even your son?"

He presses his lips together. "Not even my son."

"Listen," I start to say, and even though I've gone through this in my mind I can't seem to finish what I came to say.

"You're moving. I know."

"How?" I ask, but I already realize what he'll say. Just when I think he's going to admonish me for asking such a stupid question he comes closer and reaches for the bag. "Bob."

He raises his brow. "North Carolina, huh."

"Yes," I say.

"It gets pretty cold up there."

"It does."

He looks out toward the water. "Probably isn't too good for fishing."

"Probably not," I tell him.

"And the kids are happy?"

"They are," I say, and it's the truth. "To them it's an adventure."

He looks away. "Isn't it?"

"I suppose. Listen—I never did thank you," I tell him, and I take a deep breath. "For raising me... for teaching Brady to shoot. For a lot of things, really..."

He waves his hand in the air. "Let's not pretend I was the perfect parent. North Carolina isn't that far away..."

"I'm not pretending. If it weren't for what you did—"

"It's nothing," he tells me.

"But it wasn't nothing."

"Okay," he says. "It wasn't nothing."

~

EPILOGUE

KATE

"**W**hy'd you choose Asheville, anyway?" you ask as we deplane. I think it's because the flight atten-dant said welcome home, and the realization sort of hit us all. You usher the kids out into the aisle.

"I liked the house," I tell you, slinging my carry-on onto my shoulder.

"There are houses everywhere."

"Not like this one," I say, and it's mostly the truth but not the whole truth. What I don't tell you, not because I don't want to be honest but because I don't want to hear 'I told you so,' is that you were right. All along I thought I wanted to be like those women. I thought I wanted to 'have it all.' But having it all looks a whole lot like giving up who you are to become something someone else wants you to be. Living like that meant conforming to a standard, an ideal, a version of perfection, which wasn't real. It was an illusion no one ever really understood to begin with. It wasn't just the women, the other mothers. It was the constant aspiring that I couldn't handle. Pretty soon I looked around at my 'friends,' at our neighbors, at the rat race my life had become, and I thought, I don't want to be her, or her, or her. They're all the same, and yet, that's what I had become. I hated myself, and that's how I knew it was time to become something different. That's the beauty of this life, you get to choose. And that's what I plan to do here. Start over, where no one knows my name.

"It doesn't matter what your interests are or what you're passionate about." I said to you last night. "When you have a family, certain things have to take a backseat." You asked if I was happy, and I am. Life has its seasons, and this is the stage of life that calls for more of me. I may not get to be the ruthless, careless girl you met once upon a time. Not all the time, anyway. But she's still in there somewhere, dying to come out again, and in time, I think she will. She'll be different when she does, and with any luck, still a bit of the same. I think you'll like her. Just wait and see.

"I do like the house," you say, as you lean in and take my bag from me, always the gentleman. "But I can't say it was enough to make me move across the country."

"Okay," I relent. If you must know, then I'll tell you. You're probably bound to find out anyway. "I met someone online… it just felt right."

You consider my expression. "You met someone?" you ask and I don't like the unpleasantness in your tone.

"Yes," I answer. "In one of the mommy groups." I laugh, but nothing is funny. "And you remember that time we came here. We loved it."

You don't respond, but you study my face like you want to. Eventually you say for the umpteenth time, and I don't know why you say it now, because we're here. "I'm just not sure now was the right time to relocate."

"I know," I tell you, and I repeat your words verbatim. "The next couple of months are jam-packed."

You sigh and look out the plane window, no doubt wondering why the line isn't moving. I look at you then, really look at you.

"You've told me a million times," I remind you. "But we'll be fine. I found a great school—I have a lot on my plate, too. I'll keep busy. Really," I promise. "There's no need to worry."

You sort of nod, and thankfully the line starts to move.

~

THE DELIVERY TRUCK ARRIVES TWO HOURS LATE. I'M PREGNANT and hormonal and they're lucky they haven't arrived even a second later. I was just about ready to start digging holes in the backyard. God knows it could use a bit of fertilizer.

"Mr. And Mrs. Water?" The driver asks, looking at his clipboard, and it feels good because we've never used those aliases, not for real, not like this. Here in the Tar Heel State, we've become Jude and Kate Water. We are starting over fresh in every sense of the word, and I have to say, it feels really good to hear it confirmed out loud.

The kids are running around my legs in circles, they stop every now and again to watch the big truck, to see if our furniture has made its appearance. It hasn't. The guys are still talking to you. It's nice that our driveway here is long; it gives them plenty of room to run, and thankfully, the weather has been pretty good so far. We're coming into spring, which has always been my favorite season. Speaking of which, I wrote you a note last night thanking you for doing your best to keep the cold out all winter long. And I thanked you for being a constant reminder that spring is always right around the corner.

It's nothing, you told me later, after we'd made love. But you're wrong about that, it's everything.

Finally, the unloading starts, and I watch as they haul in

our new living room furniture. There is light at the end of the tunnel, after all, I think, and that's when she comes out, her long blonde hair flowing. It's amazing. It's everything I hoped it would be. She stops briefly to tie it up in a messy bun on top of her head. I crane my neck and watch as she slips her ear buds in. She messes with her phone, I imagine selecting the perfect song. *Turn right, I silently plead. Turn right.* I let out the breath I'd been holding when she starts jogging in our direction. It could be the pregnancy hormones, but I feel tears sting my eyes. *This is it.* When she reaches our drive, she slows, adjusts the volume on her phone, and eyes the delivery truck. The way her silhouette looks against the backdrop of the pale blue sky is like something out of a movie, and this is how I know we've come to the right place. It's perfect. The sky is cloudless, the sun is bright and blinding. But it doesn't provide much warmth. Not until I saw her, that is.

Eventually her gaze lands on me.

"Oh," she says. "I'm sorry— didn't see you there." She walks further up the drive, removing the ear buds from her ears, wrapping them around her perfect little neck. "Hello," she says to Brady. He doesn't respond. "Hi!" Olivia says in his place.

"Hi, there," she says, bending down to her level. She sticks out her hand. "I'm Melanie."

Olivia slides her hand into the woman's. "I'm Olivia," she nods. "Olivia Water."

The woman's eyes grow wide. "Where are you from, Olivia Water?"

"Oh, here and there— but mostly Texas," she says just like you taught her to. She looks up at me, proud.

"I'm Melanie," the woman says as she stands upright and holds her hand out in my direction.

"Kate," I say.

"Welcome to the neighborhood."

"We're excited to be here, more so to get settled."

She glances back at the delivery truck. "New furniture should help with that," she comments. Then she smiles, and when she does, it lights up the whole neighborhood, that smile. She's intelligent, just like I knew she'd be.

"Yeah," I say. "The buyers wanted most of our furniture. And we figured why not let 'em have it? This way, we get a fresh start, and we didn't have to lug it across the country."

She nods. "Makes sense to me."

"Do you have a daughter?" Olivia asks.

"Two," she says. "One of them is about your age, in fact."

"Can they come out and play?"

She laughs. "Later—maybe. They're out with their sitter," she says, lowering her voice. "Don't tell anybody—but I'm supposed to be working right now…"

"I won't tell," Olivia tells her and she sticks out her pinky. "Pinky promise."

"Me, either," I say. I don't offer my pinky. I figure that might be a bit much just yet.

"What do you do?" I ask, even though I know the answer.

"I'm a child psychologist," she tells me. She's proud when she says it, and I'm glad to see that she likes her job as much as I hoped she would.

"Do you see adults?" I say. "Because this move has me a little crazy."

"Not usually," she laughs. I can see that she likes my sense of humor. "But once upon a time I did."

I don't say anything to that. Mostly, I just appreciate her honesty. Also, the fact that she didn't say no.

"When is the baby due?"

"Five months," I tell her. I touch my stomach. "It just sort of popped out this week. They say that happens with your third…"

"Do you know what you're having?"

"A girl…"

"Wow," she says. "You're braver than I am."

I laugh because, we'll see. Also, because she doesn't know what a shot at redemption this is. It isn't a replacement for the daughter we lost, not by a long shot. But I would be lying if I didn't admit that it feels right.

"Well, this was kind of a surprise," I say, thinking back to the first time it hit me. Back when I vomited while putting Cheryl's body in that water. At the time, I thought I was simply overcome with emotion at having to say goodbye. That was the moment I knew we had to move. I hated to lie to you about her burial, but it needed to be special, and telling you I put her in the water would only make you worry that I hadn't done it right. Don't worry, I did. But that's not the only reason I had to get out of there. I couldn't stay in that house, in that town, knowing she wasn't in it. Not alive, anyway. It has helped being here, even more so now that Melanie and I have gotten acquainted. But I still miss her. And I still think of her everyday. In a way, this baby feels like a gift. Cheryl's way of letting me know life goes on. Not that she had anything to do with it. Obviously. But she sure did make us happy for a while, and that helped. I didn't think I wanted more kids. Now, it just feels meant to be. Plus, everyone loves a pregnant woman. Just look at Melanie here. Look how it's drawn her in.

"Surprises are the best kind," she replies, interrupting my thoughts, bringing me back to the present.

"Yes," I say, and she doesn't know how right she is.

She stretches, and I can see she's getting ready to move on. I'm not ready just yet, and apparently neither is she. She looks at me in a way that lets me know the feeling is mutual. "Anyway," she says. "I think you'll be very happy here."

"Me, too," I tell her, and then I look back at the house. You're standing on the front porch, and you look good. You look like you've belonged here all along. Her eyes follow. You wave, and I smile. "Me, too."

∽

Dear Reader,

I hope you enjoyed reading *Come Hell or High Water*. If you have a moment and you'd like to let me know what you thought, feel free to drop me an email (britney@britneyking.com).

Writing a book is an interesting adventure, but letting other people read it is like inviting them into your brain to rummage around. *This is what I like. This is the way I think.*

That feeling can be intense and interesting.

Thank you, again for reading my work. I don't have the backing or the advertising dollars of big publishing, but hopefully I have something better... readers who like the same kind of stories I do. If you are one of them please share with your friends and consider helping out by doing one (or all) of these quick things:

1. Drop me an email and let me know what you thought.
britney@britneyking.com

2. Visit my Review Page and write a 30 second review (even short ones make a big difference).

http://britneyking.com/aint-too-proud-to-beg-for-reviews/

Many readers don't realize what a difference reviews make but they make ALL the difference.

3. If you'd like to make sure you don't miss anything, to receive an email whenever I release a new title, sign up for my new release newsletter at:

https://britneyking.com/new-release-alerts/

Thanks for helping, and for reading *Come Hell or High Water.* It means a lot. Be sure to check out the second book in my latest series, *The Social Affair* at the end of this book, as well as via your favorite retailer.

Britney King

Austin, Texas

December 2017

ABOUT THE AUTHOR

Britney King lives in Austin, Texas with her husband, children, two dogs, one ridiculous cat, and a partridge in a peach tree.

When she's not wrangling the things mentioned above, she writes psychological, domestic and romantic thrillers set in suburbia.

Without a doubt, she thinks connecting with readers is the best part of this gig. You can find Britney online here:

Email: britney@britneyking.com
Web: https://britneyking.com
Facebook: https://www.facebook.com/BritneyKingAuthor
Instagram: https://www.instagram.com/britneyking_/
Twitter: https://twitter.com/BritneyKing_
Goodreads: https://bit.ly/BritneyKingGoodreads
Pinterest: https://www.pinterest.com/britneyking_/

Happy reading.

ACKNOWLEDGMENTS

First, thank you for reading my work.

To the amazing bloggers who put so much effort forth simply for the love of sharing books, many thanks.

To my editor, red ink is my favorite kind.

A special thanks to my very first readers, Samantha Wiley, Brandi Reeves, Jennifer Hanson, Nikki Reeves, and Hunter King. Thank you for making me better and for keeping me on my toes.

Thank you to the proofreading team at Proofreading By The Page.

Also, huge thanks to my advanced reader team. You all are wonderful and I couldn't be more grateful to have you on my side.

Again—because it deserves to be said twice, I'd like to thank the readers. For every kind word, for simply reading... you guys are the best.

madman hell-bent on revenge. The series has been compared to Fatal Attraction, Single White Female, and Basic Instinct.

Around The Bend

Around The Bend, is a heart-pounding standalone which traces the journey of a well-to-do suburban housewife, and her life as it unravels, thanks to the secrets she keeps. If she were the only one with things she wanted to keep hidden, then maybe it wouldn't have turned out so bad. But she wasn't.

Somewhere With You | Book One
Anywhere With You | Book Two
The With You Series Box Set

The With You Series at its core is a deep love story about unlikely friends who travel the world; trying to find themselves, together and apart. Packed with drama and adventure along with a heavy dose of suspense, it has been compared to The Secret Life of Walter Mitty and Love, Rosie.

In the tradition of *Gone Girl* and *Behind Closed Doors* comes a gripping, twisted, furiously clever read that demands your attention, and keeps you guessing until the very end. For fans of the anti-heroine and stories told in unorthodox ways, *The Social Affair* delivers us the perfect dark and provocative villain. The only question—who is it?

The Social Affair is an intense standalone about a timeless couple who find themselves with a secret admirer they hadn't bargained for. The novel explores what can happen when privacy is traded for convenience. It is reminiscent of films such as One Hour Photo and Play Misty For Me.

A timeless, perfect couple waltzes into the small coffee shop where Izzy Lewis works. Instantly enamored, she does what she always does in situations like these: she searches them out on social media.

Just like that—with the tap of a screen— she's given a front row seat to the Dunns' picturesque life. This time, she's certain she's found what she's been searching for. This time, she'll go to whatever lengths it takes to ensure she gets it right—even if this means doing the unthinkable.

Intense and original, The Social Affair is a disturbing psychological thriller that explores what can happen when privacy is traded for convenience.

"Honest to god... I'm speechless!!! This book kept me on edge through the whole story... then BAM, I was dropped was off a cliff. I LOVED IT!!!! Wow... just WOW."

THE SOCIAL AFFAIR

BRITNEY KING

COPYRIGHT

Hot Banana Press

Cover Design by Britney King LLC

Cover Image by Mario Azzi

Copy Editing by Librum Artis Editorial Services

Proofread by Proofreading by the Page

First Edition: 2018

ISBN: 978-1979057455

britneyking.com

To those who've walked into our lives without first asking permission...

PROLOGUE

A	ttachment is an awfully hard thing to break. I should
	know. I surface from the depths of sleep to complete
and utter darkness. I don't want to open my eyes. I have to. "I
warned you, and I warned you," I hear his voice say. It's not
the first time. He called out to me, speaking from the edge of
consciousness, back when I thought this all might have been
a dream. It's too late for wishful thinking now. This is his
angry voice, the one I best try to avoid. My mind places it
immediately. This one is reserved for special occasions, the
worst of times.

I hear water running in the background. Or at least I
think I do. I try to recall what I was doing before, but this is
the kind of heavy sleep you wake from and hardly know
what year you're in, much less anything else. I consider how
much time might have passed since I dozed off. Then it
hits me.

"You really shouldn't have done that," he says, and his eyes
come into focus. Those eyes, there's so much history in them;
it's all still there now. I see it reflected back to me. I read a
quote once that said… a true mark of maturity is when

someone hurts you, and you try to understand their situation instead of trying to hurt them back. This seems idealistic now. I wish someone had warned me. Enough of that kind of thinking will get you killed.

"Please," I murmur, but the rest of what I want to say won't come. It's probably better this way. I glance toward the door, thinking about what's at stake if I don't make it out of here alive, wondering whether or not I can make a break for it. It's so dark out—a clear night, a moonless sky. The power is out, I gather, and it's a fair assumption. This has always been one of his favorite ways to show me what true suffering is like. That alone would make an escape difficult. I would have to set out on foot and then where would I go? Who would believe me?

"You have it too easy," he says, as though he wants to confirm my suspicions. "That's the problem nowadays. People consume everything, appreciate nothing."

He lifts me by the hair and drags me across the bedroom. I don't have to ask why. He doesn't like to argue where he sleeps, where we make love. It's one of our safe spaces, but like many things, this too is a facade. Nothing with him is safe.

"You like your comforts, but you forget nothing good comes without sacrifice."

"I haven't forgotten," I assure him, and that much is true. Sacrifice is something I know well.

He shakes his head, careful to exaggerate his movements. He wants the message he sends to sink in. "I don't know why you have to make me so angry."

I look out toward the window, thinking I see headlights, but it's wishful thinking. Then I reach up and touch the wet spot at the crown of my head. I pull my hand away, regretful I felt the need for confirmation. Instinct is enough. If only I'd realized this sooner. I didn't have to put my fingers to it to know there would be blood; the coppery scent fills the air. "It's not too bad," he huffs as he slides one hand under my armpit and hauls me up. "Come on," he presses, his fingertips digging into my skin. "Let's get you stitched up."

I follow his lead. There isn't another option. Head wounds bleed a lot, and someone's going to have to clean his mess up. If I live, that someone will be me. *This is how you stop the bleeding.* "What time is it?"

"Oh," he says, half-chuckling. "There's no need to worry about that. She's already come and gone."

I don't ask who he's referring to. I know. I don't want him to see how deeply I am affected by what he's done. It's more dangerous this way. But what I want to happen and what actually does are two very different things. I know because my body tenses, as it gives over to emotion, eventually it seizes up completely. I don't mean for it to happen. It has a habit of betraying me, particularly where he is concerned. Your mind may know when something's bad for you. But the body can take a little longer. He knows where to touch me. He knows what to say. Automatic response is powerful, and like I said before, attachment is hard to break.

He shoves me hard into the wall. I guess I wasn't listening. I shouldn't have made a habit of that either. I don't feel the pain. I don't feel anything. "Ah, now look what you made me do," he huffs, running his fingers through his hair. He's staring at me as though this is the first time he's seeing me. His face is twisted, as though he's trying to work out his next move. He isn't. He's a planner, through and through.

Still, he's good at concealing what he doesn't want anyone to know, and if only I'd been more like that So, I don't know if this is it, if this is the end. I only know where it began.

"We had an agreement," he reminds me. And he's right.

We did have an agreement.

That's how this all started.

BRITNEY KING

∼

CHAPTER ONE

JOSIE

Two months earlier.

T he voice comes out of nowhere. I don't have to turn around to know how unfortunate this situation is. The sound is male, all male, hard and rough. Breathless and edgy. "Give me the purse," it demands. I exhale slowly. Steady my breathing. Ball my fists. Release them. Flex my fingers. *Jesus.*

I turn in disbelief, hoping I've heard wrong. The lot was empty, I know. I checked three times. Only it isn't, at least not anymore, because all of a sudden, here I am, staring down the barrel of a gun. A bad sign if there ever were one in regard to how my day might end. The man who holds it is clothed in black. Also not a good sign. He wears a ski mask that doesn't conceal his eyes, and he should know that's where the soul lives. His stance is wide, head tilted, shoulders squared. It's almost comical, save for the gun pointed at my head, like a scene straight out of a movie. He clears his throat. "I said. Give. Me. The. Purse."

I sigh and then I make a move as though I intend to slide

it from my shoulder. Thankfully, the universe isn't completely against me—a trash truck, somewhere a block or two over, slams a dumpster back to its rightful place, and for a brief second, his attention is diverted. It helps that he isn't expecting anything other than compliance. I see it in his soul.

I twist myself, position my body for maximum effect, and land a blow to his kneecap. It hits just right, and the direct hit, combined with the element of surprise, sends him down. He drops the gun in favor of his knee; that's where the hands tend to go when you inflict this level of pain from that angle. I know, I learned this where people learn most things these days: on the internet.

I take a few steps toward him, and I pick up the gun. His eyes widen as I take aim. It's a dumb move—I don't even know if it's loaded. I don't know the gun; I don't know important things—like whether the safety is on, what caliber of bullet it holds, or more importantly, what he'd have to do to make me pull the trigger. "Don't move," I order. My voice comes out calm, steadier than I feel. But then, I've had years of practice in that regard.

He puts his hands up, and then drops them so he can scoot backward.

I dig my heel into the pavement, widen my stance. "Take off the mask."

He's slow to move at first, but when I threaten to internet karate chop him again, he gets the message. He removes the mask, and this is how I know the gun is in fact loaded. I smile, thankful I made the right call.

"Better," I say.

"Please," he begs. He holds his palms upward in my direction. He wants to give me the illusion of control, even though he's bigger and stronger and likely faster. I grip the gun tighter. It's nice to have an equalizer. I'm grateful he chose a gun and not a knife because if the latter were the case, I'd have to get closer to him, giving him the advantage in the process. "Please," he says again. "I have a family."

"Most people do."

"I...I—" He begins to squirm. Nerves, I presume. That or he's trying to distract me. Neither are a good choice.

I deliver another kick, this time to the opposite kneecap, just to ensure he doesn't move. Then I fish the Altoid I had been digging for from my pocket and slip it onto my tongue. *One should always come prepared.* He's whimpering, writhing on the ground, shuffling back and forth from his right side to his left. His pained expression makes him look younger than he is. With his curly hair and jet-black eyes, he isn't unattractive. It makes me wonder what would have to happen in a person's life to make it come to this.

Slowly, I take three steps backward. And then one more just to be sure. "It's almost Christmas," I say. "What are you thinking, robbing people at a time like this?"

He looks at me strangely. Christmas means nothing to him. Also, he thinks I'm an idiot. Christmas, or any other time, really—thieves aren't selective— is the perfect time to steal what isn't yours. People are distracted. They let their guards down, all too willing to believe in what's good. I realize this now.

"Do you know what could have happened if I'd given you my purse?"

He furrows his brow and considers my question. He's expecting a sob story. I don't look as desperate as I am. Eventually, his face twists as though I'm crazy, and today he isn't wrong. Finally, he shakes his head.

"I might have wound up dead. That is—if you didn't kill me first."

"I'm sorry," he says. But it's a lie, only as sincere as the predicament in which he's now found himself.

"Give me one reason I shouldn't pull the trigger..."

He doesn't immediately answer me, and this makes me nervous. Every second counts. I've learned this lesson well. "It's not like it wouldn't be self-defense."

"My grandma," he says, finally. Before he starts huffing and hawing about his knees again.

"Your grandma." I tilt my head. I hadn't expected that.

"Yeah, I look after her. She's blind and bedridden."

"What does that have to do with me?"

"If I don't go home, no one will find her. Not for days...."

I reposition the gun, lower it slightly and then raise it again. I look down the barrel and line up the sight. Then I squeeze one eye shut the way they do in the movies. "I don't believe you."

He starts waving his hands. This is his problem in life, I can see. No one taught him how to use words to get what he wants, so he resorts to violence. "She has diabetes. I need the money for insulin."

I study him carefully. He has a sense of desperation about him. And not just because I have a gun pointed at his heart. I read about that on the internet, too. Where to aim. Makes it hard to miss. Anyway, I know the look, and somehow I think he might be telling the truth, which makes this situation all the more sad.

"Fine," I say. "But prison is going to cost you a lot more than insulin." I know as the words leave my mouth what I'm saying isn't altogether true. If he is in fact telling me the truth, not getting the insulin his grandmother needs would have far greater effects than knowing he did what he could and went to jail for it. Either way, he failed. But in his mind, in the latter scenario, at least he would know he'd given it his all. Street credit. That's his currency.

I watch as he shifts onto his side. He's slow and careful about it and still I make sure the gun is trained on him. He reaches into his pocket, and I learn quick— there's no safety. "Make another move and you're dead."

"Wait," he calls out, and it's a piece of paper he's retrieved, not a weapon. "See—it's her prescription."

"Keep your hands where I can see them," I say. It's cliché. I feel it as the words float off into the breeze. *Look how cliché you've become, Josie.* But I have to admit, when your life is at stake, sometimes it's the most logical thing to say.

I take two more steps backward. It surprises him when I throw my purse at him. He ducks and covers his head.

"In the right pocket, there's a hundred-dollar bill. Get it out."

His eyes narrow; he's confused. He reaches for it and pulls it toward him anyway.

"Not that one," I nod. "The small pocket."

He digs. I look up at the sky and notice the big puffy clouds, the kind the kids and I used to spend hours staring at. We imagined they were dragons and dinosaurs, angels and other things too. I wish I could go back. Back to a time when I wasn't where I am now, back against the wall, back to when things were idyllic and stable. Even if it was all a facade. You can't know that you don't want to know a thing until you already know it. Once it's there, you can't erase it. It's interesting; you don't realize how you'll miss stability, predictability even, until the rug is pulled out from under you.

"Got it," he calls out. I hear relief in his tone, and I know I will regret this later. There will be hell to pay. I also know I shouldn't reward a kid who just tried to rob me. But when you're down on your luck, sometimes it's good to know others have it worse. Plus, it would have been really bad if I'd had to explain where I was when I lost my purse. I should count my blessings.

I cock my head. "Slide the purse back."

He does, and I use my foot to inch it closer, keeping the gun on him.

"You almost shot someone's mother. I hope you think about that tonight when you're drifting off to sleep."

He doesn't say anything. I can see he doesn't know what to say.

"Oh—and you're going to want to ice those kneecaps."

"Thank you…" he says, shoving the money in his pocket.

"And by the way, I'm keeping this," I tell him, holding the gun up.

He sighs heavily, and I can see his weapon was hard to come by. This is both bad and good. Good because it shows he won't easily be able to get a replacement. Bad because it tells me he needs one. "Turn around." I use the gun to motion him in the direction I want him to go.

He scoots around, going counter-clockwise. "Don't get up until you no longer hear my engine. Otherwise—I'll turn right back around and hold you here until the cops show up."

"Okay."

I bite my lip. It hits me then. The answer to my questions might very well be right in front of me. *The simplest answer's usually the right one.* "Let me ask you a question…"

He glances over this shoulder.

I tilt my head. "Do you think one has a moral obligation to stop something horrible from happening to another person?"

His eyes narrow. He thinks I'm referring to this situation. He thinks I'm referring to him. "I don't know."

"You know what I think?"

He juts out his bottom lip and shakes his head.

"I think most people would say yes."

He shrugs again. "Sounds very philosophical. Where I come from they don't teach much of that."

"Life teaches you," I say.

He watches me carefully.

"But what if that person wronged them? Does the rule still apply?"

"Rules are rules." He doesn't believe his own lie.

"What about karma? Survival of the fittest?"

"I think karma has a way of working itself out. I don't really think you have to help it along…"

It's the first intelligent thing he's said. But he's wrong. Sometimes you do have to help it along. Alternatively, sometimes, and as luck would have it, in his case, you decide to just let it be.

"Turn around."

He does as I ask. But first, I see the confusion on his face. It's mixed with a bit of terror. He isn't completely convinced I won't put a bullet in the back of his head. It's better this way.

I wait for a second just to make sure he continues to face the opposite direction. When I'm reasonably confident he's going to comply, I remind him one last time. "Stay." I start backward, carefully, meticulously, toward the safety of my car.

He scoffs. He's not used to being told what to do. This is how it all starts. If only parents could press a fast-forward button, if they could see into the future, then this kid might've had a chance. Now, karma is going to work itself out, and in his case, it's just a matter of time.

"Eyes straight ahead," I remind him once I've reached my car. I don't want him getting a look at my license plate. I've scared him. But probably not enough. Retribution can be a bitch. I should know.

That's why I was here in the first place.

≈

Learn more at: britneyking.com

58138124R00142